FAMILY MATTERS

MORTALITY BITES SERIES

RAMY VANCE

KEEP EVOLVING STUDIOS

To my Astarte - I love you

FAMILY MATTERS

PART I
A BEGINNING OF SORTS

I was turned into a vampire on my fifteenth birthday. Happy birthday, Kat Darling—or rather, Happy *undead*-day. At the time—so long ago—I was young enough to still need my parents, but old enough to find them embarrassing.

Now, three hundred years later—give or take a decade—I'm nineteen (well, *three hundred* and nineteen), human again and still embarrassed of my mom.

I guess some things never change.

To be fair, even if I weren't a few centuries old (a few centuries undead?), I think I'd be embarrassed of her. I mean, who wouldn't? Enter a woman in her early forties, wearing a nearly fluorescent purple skirt and matching blazer, with a scarf that must have been purchased from Harrods in the 1930s, oversized sunglasses that would have suited a young Audrey Hepburn, round, chipmunk cheeks of a woman past her heyday and long, clearly dyed blond hair tied in a bun so tight I keep expecting her hairline to disappear when the roots snap free from her scalp.

Can you imagine? Being seen next to someone like that?

Alas. Can't choose your family, I suppose. All that could be forgiven, too, if she wasn't standing right here, right now, in the foyer of the Other Studies Library, yelling my name at the top of her smoked-out lungs.

"KATRINA!"

This must be my punishment for everything I did as a vampire, I thought as I looked for a hole to crawl in and die.

I smelled Obsession for Women and menthol cigarettes a full three seconds before she ran over and hugged me, wiping away a tear.

"Darling, *darling.* How is my Katrina Darling?" She laughed at her own joke. I don't know why—it wasn't as if she hadn't said it, oh I don't know, a million times before. When I didn't laugh—and no one else did—she summoned every ounce of her motherly melodrama, looked around the room at the students trying to study and said, "It's funny because her name is Katrina Darling. Get it? *Darling,* darling?"

A few students gave her a sympathy chuckle before—embarrassed for the stranger with the unfortunate name and even more unfortunate mother—shoving their noses back into their books.

"Mommm," I said, shocked that after all these centuries I still used the same wary tone that was one part begging, two parts death-inviting embarrassment. Was that how I sounded on my fifteenth birthday so long ago? "Stop it, please. You're making a scene."

"Pish, posh," she said, a fake upper-class British accent punctuating the words like faux crystal. "Come here and give your old Mama another hug!" And before I could protest, she wrapped her arms around me and pulled me in. Tight. I gagged on the smell.

And I mean *really* tight. I tried to break free, but she wasn't letting go. For a moment I thought that she really missed me—that this embrace was a long-overdue connection after years of being enemies and then decades of being estranged. Should have known better. "Older and wiser" doesn't apply to the undead, even if they do come back to life.

Can you blame me? I began to lean into the embrace, remembering what it was like to be a pre-teen and needing Mom to chase away the bad dreams or fix up a scraped knee. Remembering how she could make everything OK when we were human—

4

And then she destroyed it all by whispering in my ear, "I fear, darling, that you and I are in danger." She pulled away and gave me that serious look of hers, the one she'd given whenever she "meant business," and added, "*Both* of us are in danger, darling."

Good ol' Mom. Well, at least good ol' pre- and now post-vampire Mom. When she was turned, she became the Queen Bitch. Heartless, ruthless, selfish. And even though her own daughter was a vampire, too, and the two of us could have had an eternity together, she didn't seem to care. I was a drag on her new undead life. So she walked away from me the second she could.

And now that she was back? It was because she was in danger and needed my help—or so she claimed.

But that was Mom. Always looking out for herself. So why was I so surprised?

Mom pulled away and leveled a heavy gaze at me. "*Excuse* me, darling?"

Damn it—talking out loud again. Nasty habit, that. It came from centuries of haunting an old Scottish castle up in the highlands. When you spent 99% of your time alone, you tended to keep yourself company—which usually meant talking to yourself. Old habits died hard, just like me.

"Nothing, Mother," I said, trying to throw in as much disappointment as I could. I wanted her to *hear* my eyeroll. I was becoming—or rather *reverting*—to a right stroppy teenager. Good. She missed those years anyway, so why not give her a dose now?

"I'm serious, darling. We are in grave danger. And given that neither you nor I have our old"—she looked around to see if anyone was listening and then leaned in to whisper—"*abilities*, I think we best find a place to speak."

I nodded. She was serious. There was a danger—to her, at least. I doubted *I* was in danger. If history were anything to judge by—and we had plenty of it to judge—she was the only one truly in danger and was about to use me to save herself. In fact, she probably put me in danger by coming here.

Not that she cared that her daughter was in harm's way. She never was the kind of person to say, "Go on without me," or "Stay away, I'll only bring you harm." She was more of a, "Get me out of here! Carry me if you have to!" kind of gal.

Still ... she was my mom. Blood thicker than water, or whatever (that expression kind of lost its meaning when I started drinking blood as a snack). Plus, I owed her for—

"Darling, you're doing that thing you always do."

Pulled out of my own thoughts, I shook my head and, clamping my jaws tight so I wouldn't speak even the body language out loud, shrugged a *What are you talking about?*

"That thousand-mile stare of yours as you contemplate some random thought. You know—that you're pretending to listen even though anyone with half a brain knows you're not." She tucked a loose strand of hair behind my ear as she spoke and then adjusted my collar. I knew it was all a show.

I pulled away, pretending not to like her touch, when really, if I were honest with myself (and that's something I'm really trying to do lately, promise), I enjoyed it and longed for more.

"OK, *fine.* I'll listen. Let's find somewhere quiet to talk," I said, and led her away from the main study area to the little museum that was in the back of the library.

Great start to a family reunion.

↔

Once we were in the back area, I lifted a hand to my ear and pushed it toward her. "OK, I'm listening."

She shook her head and gave me a tisk of the tongue as she walked to the back display. "You don't have to be so snarky, darling."

"I don't?" I said, imbuing the words with as much snark as I could muster.

"No, you don't. I know that we've had our differences, but—"

"You tried to kill me. Not once, not twice—but more times than I have nails to paint."

"When we were *vampires*, darling. Not as a human. *Never* as a human. Besides, you have to admit that I was only trying to … you know …" She let the words hang in the air for a moment before waving a hand like she was waving away some smoke. "But that's all history now. History, and water under the bridge. Let's let bygones be bygones and all that good stuff," she said as she continued to the back of the display area.

I knew where she was going, but I followed anyway. It really was like riding a bike, this mother-daughter thing—not that I knew much about riding a bike; it had been decades since I'd tried, and that expression never really cut it for me. But still. It was almost good to have my mother back.

Once at the back she pointed at a large framed costume—a kilt complete with fur sporran and Brogue shoes—before stopping. "They put it up for display for all to see," she said in a voice dripping with accusation, then, pulling out a tissue from her gaudy, golden purse, raised her sunglasses so she could dab the corners of her eyes.

I genuinely couldn't tell if she was actually wiping away tears, or if this were some melodrama to elicit sympathy from me.

"Do you know how many times I had to sew that kilt for your father?" she said. "He was always snagging it on some branch or fence or whatever while doing his chores. So clumsy, that father of yours. I wonder who fixed it after I was …" Her voice trailed off to nothing again, and dab-dab came the tissue.

She didn't need to finish for me to know what she meant. *After I turned you into a vampire,* I thought, pausing to make sure I was actually saying it in my head and not out loud. I was—thank the Gone-Gods for small miracles. I would have finally died from the awkwardness if she'd heard me say that.

I walked over to the display and touched the glass, and a flood of unwelcome memories assaulted my already overtaxed brain. Memories like the one of my fifteenth birthday. Turned into a vampire at an age where I was still young enough to need my family. A young, frightened girl not wanting to be alone, turning to my mom. And *turning* my mom.

Then I tried to turn my dad, too, but he refused, fighting me off like I was some sort of demon.

And I was.

It would have been fine if it had ended there, but he became obsessed with hunting my mother and me. He even formed his own clan—the Divine Cherubs—where members wore cherub masks (in other words, baby masks—they looked ridiculous) and hunted vampires. Just vampires at first, and then all sorts of demons as time progressed.

Over the years I saw my father turn into legend, then myth. Amongst those who had brushes with demons, dark magic and other clandestine members of the Underworld, my father was a hero and symbol of what was good and right.

But of course that was centuries ago when mythical creatures— good and evil—were hidden from humans. A time when most believed that beings like dragons, fairies, angels, devils and vampires were just the stuff of stories, old wives' tales.

That all changed, of course, about four years ago when the gods left, their last message to the world being a voice broadcast for all the world to hear: "Thank you for believing in us, but it's not enough. We're leaving. Good luck."

The second that "Good luck" rang in our collective heads, the skies and ground and oceans and just about everything else opened up, and out came all those mythical beings that no one really believed in—out in the open for everyone to see. It was raining cats and dogs and angels and trolls and everything in between.

I wish this were the setup for some joke, but my dorm roommate is a changeling. That's it. No punchline. As in creature-of-nature, fae-warrior-with-a-broadsword, *changeling*. But who was I to act surprised? I was a vampire.

Was being the operative word. Seems that when the gods left, not only were we overrun with creatures once thought of as legend, but their departure also altered the way magic worked.

For one thing, creatures with magical talent now had to exchange bits of their life-force to get their mojo working. In other words, should a valkyrie wish to cast a fireball or a tunda wish to shapeshift, they would have to give up a bit of their life to make it happen. A week, maybe a month. Creatures once immortal—they call themselves OnceImmortals, original, right?—are terrified of death, and would need a very good reason to give up a second of life—let alone longer.

The other change to how magic worked was half-breeds—beings that were half-human, half-something else—reverted back to being fully human. Werewolves, werehyenas, weredragons, were-whatever —human. Zombies and ghouls—human.

Vampires? Human.

"I wonder where his mask is …" my mother said.

I blinked, coming back to reality. "Mask? Oh, mask … you mean his cherub's mask. It's, ahhh, in the back, I think. Being cleaned."

"And his dirk?"

"Ah, yeah, that too. Real nasty, it was."

She gave me a look that said she didn't believe me. And she was right not to. Both items were currently hidden in my dorm room. They probably did need a good cleaning, though.

I grabbed her hand and pulled her away from the display to distract from my lie. "You said something about danger?"

"I did—it seems that we're being hunted."

"By who?"

"By *whom*, darling. Don't tell me that the centuries undid the classical education your father and I gave you." She gave me an appraising look. And by appraising, I mean, a 'this item is broken and therefore requires a discount' kind of thing. Then she shrugged and sighed before going on, "Not sure yet. All I know for sure is that we're being hunted by the same people."

"Who?"

"*Whom.* Like I said, I'm not sure."

Well, this sounded promising. "Why are we being hunted? Unless you're not sure of that either."

"Oh, I'm very sure of the *why*. You for a different reason than me."

9

"Which is …?"

She sighed, looked into the nearest display and said, "Not here, darling. Let us go for a walk."

It was my turn to sigh. And this time I really did roll my eyes.

Good ol' Mom.

1

IN CASE YOU HAVEN'T HEARD— THE GODS ARE GONE

*M*y mother and I left the relative quiet and security of the near-empty Other Studies Library for the hustle and bustle on lower campus. It was a large open area between the university libraries, the buildings that housed the Science, Arts and Business classes, and Student Admin. To the south was the university's main entrance and city.

This was my home: McGill University. It was one of the few universities that accepted Other submissions, and the only place of higher education that had an entire library dedicated to the study of Others. Everyone else that studied Others tended to do so in military bunkers.

This particular spot on lower campus was where everyone gathered between classes to play Ultimate frisbee, pretend to study, smooch (how 1930s of me) and just generally hangout. For some reason that predates me (as a human student, that is), everyone calls this area The Quad.

For the life of me, I have no idea why. My best guess is that some *Star Trek* geek pointed out that it was in fact shaped in quadrants (*quad* for short, obviously) where everyone was supposed to divide into cliques, and it caught on.

I don't mind. I have to admit ... I do love *Star Trek.*

On the grassy fields stood every manner of student this GoneGod World had to offer. Humans, dracons, yetis, fairies, pixies, houri, raiju, baku and clurichaun all hung around, either waiting for their next call or ditching a class in favor of some fun in the sun.

It was good to see so many different species getting along, to be honest. Not three months ago, an old librarian (the guy who used to be in charge of the Other Studies Library, and a bit of a friend) was killed, and one of the mythical creatures—an Other—was, of course, blamed. This nearly caused a civil war between Others and humans, but thankfully things got sorted out when it was proven that a human was behind the killing.

Still, it could have been bad—

"Darling, you're muttering to yourself."

"I am? Er, I am," I said, silently admonishing myself for talking out loud again. My mother was giving me that disapproving look she gave when I was doing something she didn't like, but wasn't bad enough to outright punish, much to her chagrin. Like eating my vegetables too slow for her liking.

But her eyes (paradoxically, she'd stowed her sunglasses in her purse as soon as we stepped into the sun; but when a vampire has missed the sun for three hundred years, you tended to stop trying to hide from it) also betrayed that she hadn't quite heard me. She'd heard something, but not everything, and it clearly vexed her. Her old age was finally catching up to her.

"What was I saying?" I asked, both to know what she'd heard and vex good ol' Mom a wee bit more. What can I say? Daughters—we're a handful.

"Something about Others and humans getting along. I don't know, sounds like a load of crock to me. You know, darling, ever since you became a part of this new world and lost your Scottish accent, I find you difficult to follow. Breaks your mother's heart."

" 'Became a part of this new world' ... interesting choice of words. But what do you mean exactly? The Americas or the GoneGod world?"

12

I wince at hearing myself say that. I hated how she referred to this entire continent as the *Americas*. But she comes by that word honestly—it was the term used in our time. I let it slip by habit, which was becoming a … habit … around this woman.

"Both—but mostly I mean the GoneGod World." She stopped walking and turned to me, taking my hand. "Oh darling, I'm falling into old habits of not saying what I mean and still wanting you to understand me. I am so sorry."

Old habits. Like mother, like daughter, I suppose?

She took my hand in hers and for a long moment, I stared at it, not sure what to do. In the three hundred years and change we'd both been vampires, we were constantly at each other's throats—literally—always trying to hurt one another with words and with teeth.

And here I was—newly human and holding the hand of the woman who both gave me life and tried to take it back.

But that wasn't the most confusing part. She'd just apologized. To me. Without me holding an axe to her neck (long story). She never apologized. Not as a human and certainly not as a vampire.

Although my brain told me that this was an act, my heart said it wasn't. I know my heart—after three hundred years you get to know yourself in a way no self-help book or shrink could do for you—and it both told me what I *should* believe and what I *wanted* to believe.

Trouble with *should* and *want* is that neither of them mean *true*.

Still. I clasped down on her hand and said, "So what do you mean?"

"I mean *me*, darling. Me. I'm the one who is struggling with this new GoneGod World. Ever since I lost my powers, I've just been … floundering. Before I could hear your every thought, whether you were speaking out loud or not. Now, I can barely hear you when you are standing right next to me." She scanned the Quad. "I could sense danger before it was anywhere near me, I could hardcore-parkour myself from here to the top of that building without breaking a sweat."

"Hardcore parkour?" I asked. She'd clearly picked that up from a college kid on the way to the library.

She ignored me. "I could see a bee's ass from five hundred meters away. Now I can't do any of that. I'm just ... just ..."

"Human?"

She nodded, pulled away her hand and dug into her purse, finding a cigarette. Lighting it, she inhaled a deep breath and slowly blew out a menthol-filled puff of smoke. She calmed down, whether with the nicotine, menthol, simple act of smoking or all three.

"Mom," I said in soft voice that surprised even me. "You shouldn't smoke—those things will kill you."

"Oh darling, darling," she laughed, "you always did care for others. Must've gotten that from your father." Then, looking at the cigarette as if appraising a diamond, she sighed. "Alas, I just can't kick it, darling. I have been smoking for nearly two centuries without consequences ... and now that there are consequences, I frankly don't give a damn."

"You could vape," I offered.

She gave me a blank look that simultaneously conveyed that she didn't understand what I meant, nor did she care too. I let it go. I was used to that look.

"I get what you mean," I said. "To lose all that strength ... all our abilities. But it's not all bad."

She tilted her head, narrowing her eyes, challenging me to prove it.

"For one thing," I said, "we can get our food from a grocery store instead of ... you know." I made a chomping noise.

She raised one eyebrow, as if to say that wasn't a positive life change at all.

I added, "For another thing, we're standing outside. In the sun. Together."

At that she looked up at the sun and smiled. "True. So very true." Then her face went somber again. "Darling, I'm afraid I have put you in grave danger by being here ... and if I had any other choice I would have stayed a million miles away."

"So you've mentioned. Can you tell me what this is about?"

"The gods are gone."

"I know," I said, feeling my old teenage anger flaring up at my mom's ability to state the obvious and prattle on without actually saying anything at all.

"Ever wonder where they went?"

"No, not really. Golf resort? I just figured that the gods were being selfish pricks by going and causing all this trouble."

My mom, a devout Catholic despite the Scotland of her childhood being Presbyterian, would have never let me get away with using the word "god," or even "gods," and "prick" in the same sentence.

But instead of the expected tirade, she just nodded. "*You* might not have wondered or cared, but do you think that is true of those around you?" She gestured at my fellow students on the Quad.

I looked over the crowd of Others and humans and knew that most would love to know where the gods went. Their departure—their GrandExodus (who names these things?)—was so sudden, and the appearance of the Others was so unexpected, that the world was thrown into chaos. And even though this university had opened up admissions to all species, I knew I was living in a bubble.

Elsewhere, people were suffering. Violence had never been higher, and was only rising. People were dying. And all because their once loved gods didn't care enough about them to stick around and keep the world in line.

I was sure that many would want to know where the gods went. And why they left. Not because the knowledge would change anything, but because it would offer some semblance of closure. Perhaps even peace.

Returning my gaze to my mother, I nodded. "I suppose many would want to know."

"And what would that knowledge—if it fell into the wrong hands—do?"

"I'm not sure I know what you mean."

"Think about it, darling. If some master manipulator or fantastic liar were to get this knowledge, can you imagine the harm they could do? Force people into believing something that isn't true. Develop a new religion based on getting the gods back—or keeping them away forever. Force Earth's resources into developing technology to follow the gods to whatever golf resort they fled to."

I stared at her, not responding.

She forged on. "Use it as leverage to take control, darling. *That* is the power of that knowledge—of the greatest unanswered question—should it fall into the wrong hands."

At first, my natural inclination was to insist that she was wrong, that she was just being dramatic. But as soon as my knee-jerk, parents-don't-know-anything reaction subsided, I thought about what she said carefully and couldn't deny that she was absolutely right. There is no telling what Others and humans alike could be manipulated into doing or believing if they knew where their gods went.

And knowing where they went was one step before knowing *why* they left. *Why* was far more dangerous than *where*. *Why* would carry all sorts of implications with it—we weren't good enough, devoted enough, powerful enough. Entire cults had already sprung up, either to atone for driving the gods away or to appease them enough to return, or, in some cases, with a level of cognitive dissonance only achievable by religious nuts, somehow both. And all of it was built on baseless speculation.

Give them a reason that was real and—

I shook my head. "I doubt most would believe them."

"Ahhh, you were always a sharp one, my dear. But what if I told you that we could not only find out where they went, but also verify the absolute truth in that knowledge. This isn't a 'maybe' or 'possibly' scenario. This is a without-a-shadow-of-a-doubt situation."

"How?"

"Magic, darling. *Magic*."

"Magic comes with a price."

"But think of the knowledge, darling. Knowledge, mind you, that would have proof behind it. Knowledge that would be absolutely verifiable. I know it's a lot to take in. But it's true. And what's more," my mother said, leveling me with an ominous stare, "you have the key to unlocking this knowledge."

2

DANGER, LOST GODS AND BOYFRIENDS

What a load of centaur shit.

"You're thinking out loud again, darling."

I glared at my mother. Good ol' Mom, piquing my interest despite myself. "Key?"

"Well, from what I understand it's more like an amulet—"

"OK, OK, slow down for a second," I said, trying to remind myself that I was staring at a woman who had done a heck of lot of evil in her life. Granted, all of that was as a vampire, and she was human now—as far as I could tell—but I had once been a vampire, too, and I can honestly say with firsthand knowledge that losing your soul doesn't change who you are.

Not entirely.

It just removes the consequences of your actions, which in time whittles away your guilt. After all, if you were going to live forever and it was virtually impossible to kill you, why care about what you do? And what's more, if all that power depended on you sucking some blood out of normal people who didn't have any power—well, after a few decades, you start to have as much regard for them as one might a slab of steak bought from a grocery store (and before you ask—I have never met a vegetarian vampire, partly because blood is simply too tempting, but mostly because if you didn't drink, you didn't live).

A slab of meat ... yikes. Sorry for the visual.

Anyway, now that I'm human again, I really don't feel that different. Sure, I don't need blood and I'm no longer super-strong, super-fast or super-*anything*. But it's more than that. It's not like my personality changed. Well, *completely*, anyway.

That's the hardest part about being human now. Deep down you always knew killing was wrong, but you did it anyway. You did it because when given the choice between killing and dying, you chose killing. And now all that blood followed you around in life, and this time it wouldn't quench your thirst.

That was what it was like for me.

But my mother—she was something else. Some*one* else. Free of consequences she did as she liked when she liked, no matter who was hurt, and she never blinked an eye weighed down with an ounce of remorse. At least that's what I saw.

Thinking all this and still trying to find my mom's angle, I said, "So you're one of the good guys ... trying to keep the amulet out of the bad guys' hands."

"Oh darling, you always ask the question behind the question. You should be asking how it is that you have the key—"

"Kat. Kat!"

I didn't need to turn around to know who it was. I could recognize that Ghanaian's voice in the middle of a hurricane.

"Hi, Egya," I said, not turning around.

Caught at college with my mother. How embarrassing.

↔

"Kat, where have you been? You missed Psych class."

My eyes opened wide and I think my pupils must have shrunk

because my mom put a concerned hand on my shoulder. "Shit," I muttered.

"We reviewed for Tuesday's test. Lots of good information," Egya said, his white teeth accented by his dark skin. Tall, muscular and handsome, Egya had all the signs of a strong, stable man. Then he spoke and almost everything that came out of his mouth was a joke or game.

But me missing Psychology 101 was no joke. I was barely passing the class and if I didn't get at least a C on the test I'd flunk and be forced to repeat it or change majors. Right now that didn't seem like a bad thing—why did you need Psychology in Business School, anyway?

"I totally forgot ..." I started.

Egya ignored me, pushing past and extending his hand to my mother, his voice suddenly as formal as Cinderella's ball. "Hello, Ms. Darling—I am Egya-Boi Awoonar. Katrina's classmate, friend and person who bails her out with his most excellent notes."

My mother clasped his hand and instead of shaking it, he turned her wrist so that the palm faced downward and kissed the back of her hand.

"What a charmer," my mom said.

Without missing a beat, he said, "You must be Katrina's mother. I would have gone with the classic line that you are her sister, but that would have been disingenuous. I suspect you are far too refined a woman to fall for such overused platitudes. So instead, I will ask what it was like to have a daughter so young."

"A *real* charmer." My mother's smile touched the corners of her eyes. "I am, and I *did* have her young. Very young. And none of this 'Ms. Darling.' Please call me Charlie, or CC for short."

"Very well, Charlie—what brings you to such juvenile surroundings as a college quad?"

I noted that they were still holding hands. I also noted that as charming as Egya could be, this was clearly just a show to annoy me. Egya was a werehyena (well, an ex-werehyena), and hyenas, I'd come to learn during my friendship with Egya, really did love to play their games.

This game was that he knew full well about my strained relationship with my mother. He knew all about my father, and how he died. Truth be told, Egya was one of three people on campus who knew pretty much my entire bloody past. So he knew how uncomfortable I was in this moment—and played his games anyway. Or maybe *because* I was uncomfortable. Freaking werehyenas.

I had to admit, though ... that was what I both hated and loved about him. And when he gave me a knowing wink, I couldn't help but tip the scales more toward love.

OK—so Egya and my mom talking was bad, but manageable. Now I just had to get them apart and I'd be—

"Kat!" I heard another voice call out.

I turned to see a tall boy with lush, black hair and impossibly blue eyes trot toward us.

GoneGodDammit!

My boyfriend too.

↔

"And who is this tall drink of water?" my mom said, leering way too much for comfort.

"Ahhh, Mother—this is Justin. He's my, ahh ... friend."

Justin winced at this, and to my continued horror he didn't recover quick enough for it to go unnoticed. My mother, being my mother, gave him a sultry smile that I'd seen her use on drunken sailors and horny construction workers alike and said, " 'Friend'? Darling ... swoop this one up, lest I do."

At this, Justin's wince turned into a scarlet blush.

My cheeks turned red, too—but not out of embarrassment.

"OK, guys—thank you for saying hello, but my mother and I are catching up and so, you know—"

"Nonsense, darling. I am so pleased to meet your friends," she hissed, the *s* in *pleased* lingering a bit too long for my liking.

"But Mother—we were discussing *important matters* and I really think we should finish up."

My mother, not taking her eyes off Justin, nodded. "I fear Ms. Practicality and fruit-of-my-loins is right."

Both Justin and Egya laughed at this, but I was happy to hear it sounded less sincere and more polite.

"We must continue our discussions," my mother finally conceded. "But that doesn't stop us from meeting for dinner. Say, eight-ish?"

"And I know just the place," Egya said. "There's a new diner across the street from the old abandoned theatre: Mama's. Supposed to have the best poutine in the city."

"Poutine?" my mother said, lifting an eyebrow.

"Oh, you are in for a treat, Ms. Da ... ah, I mean Charlie."

"Then it is settled. Justin and Egya will join us at Mama's. *Mama's* ... fitting name given our recent reunion, don't you think, Katrina?"

Gritting my teeth—lest I resume my old habit of biting—I nodded.

↔

With dinner plans in place, I shooed Justin and Egya away. The Ghanaian left with a chuckle after handing me a photocopy of his Psychology notes (good guy, that Egya), but Justin wasn't so easy to push away. He wanted a kiss goodbye, I could see it in his eyes—but as much as I love Justin's lips on mine, I wasn't going to do that in front of my mom. Too much fodder for her to use against me later. So instead I gave him an awkward, impersonal kiss on the cheeks—both of them—and walked away.

I'm going to pay for that later, I thought—unfortunately out loud.

"Indeed you are," my mom agreed.

↔

With them finally gone, I turned to my mother and, not hiding my anger, said, "No more games. *Danger,* you said. Where? When?"

"The amulet, dear? The key? Don't you want to know how it is you have it?"

"The museum," I said, shrugging.

My mom lifted an impressed eyebrow.

"I don't own any amulets, Mom. The museum has several. It was the only obvious place it could be. Not that hard to guess. Now—the danger. These bad people who want it ... where are they and when are they showing up?"

She crossed her arms and sniffed. "All business. Just like your father, I see."

I didn't respond, just stared at her until she finally caved and answered my question.

"I don't know when, all I know is that if I could track the amulet to this place, then so can they. Intel says they are currently unaware of the amulet, so it could be some time. The important thing is to retrieve it and wipe out any record that it was here so that they never come."

" 'Intel'?" I chuckled at the word. The mother I knew would never use a word like *intel.* It was too hokey, too much of an abbreviation. A part of me wondered how she'd react if she knew "Quad" was an abbreviation, too. She was more of a "My people say ..." or "A little birdie told me ..."

Intel. I stared at her. My mother was acting so different, so bizarre, that it was hard for me to believe this was the same person I'd known for three centuries. And then it dawned on me that maybe she wasn't being honest. Should have been obvious, really, but I was letting that small part of me that still wanted a mother cloud my judgment.

"What's your angle, Charlie? Someone paying you to retrieve it? One of the bad guys, perhaps?"

My mother put a hand on her chest and gave me a faux hurt look. "Darling, I would—"

"Save it. The truth."

She kept her hand on her heart, her face frozen in mock indignation. Then, perhaps realizing she'd lost, she sighed and nodded. "Very well. I work for an organization whose sole purpose is to keep the peace between Others and humans. When we learned the amulet was here, at your University, they tasked me with retrieving the amulet because, well, of our history."

"If they had any brains, they would have sent someone I didn't know."

Now my mom gave a real hurt look and I knew I had gotten to her. It felt amazing.

"Yes, perhaps. But as soon as I knew you were a part of this, I asked to come. I wanted an excuse to see you and figured that if I just showed up, you'd push me away."

"You *did* just show up."

She charged on. "But if I came on an important mission … like I said—I see so much of your father in you. And before you say anything else—yes, I'm being paid. Like I said, it's my job."

I scanned my mother's face, looking for any hint of a lie, and saw none. She was telling the truth. Or at least, she *thought* she was telling the truth. What's the expression? The road to Hell is paved with good intentions. If that were true, my mother had an expressway named after her.

↔

"OK—what's the plan?" I asked.

"Retrieve the amulet. Have dinner. Leave," she said in a matter-of-fact way.

I shook my head. "Have dinner. Prove to me that you really are working for the good guys. Retrieve amulet. Leave."

"Proof? Would a phone call suffice?"

"From who?"

"*Whom*, darling, from *whom*."

I gritted my teeth. "From … whom?"

She smiled. "Why, the President."

"Make it a FaceTime, and maybe …"

3

DORM ROOMS, CHANGELINGS
AND CALCULUS

I never got FaceTime with the President—probably for the best. I did, however, get routed through several very official-sounding guys all assuring me that my mother worked for them. They used acronyms and lofty terms like "assets," "divulge" and "clearance" practically every third word and I just couldn't imagine my mother going through all that trouble just to trick me.

Then again ... this was the same woman who once turned the captain of an Aircraft Carrier just so she could—as she put it—*travel the oceans in style*. After talking to several more people with even more inventive jargon, I decided to—maybe, cautiously, grain-of-salty—believe my mother.

I dropped my mom off at her hotel—which was the closest possible hotel to the University Dorms, I noted—and went home to regroup. If I was going to survive dinner tonight, I needed some *me* time.

Sadly, *me* time is virtually impossible when your roommate is a changeling.

The first time I met Deirdre, she was standing butt-naked in our room, trying to staple AstroTurf onto our dorm walls. Being a child of nature (and not in the hippie, let's-all-get-along way, but in the literal

Mother Nature sense), she needed to have the natural world around her.

I kind of thought of her like a penguin. They can live on land, but need to be by the ocean to live. Deirdre was my penguin, and today I came home to find her sitting on the floor, wearing the crawler vines we attached to our wall for a dress, nursing baby—

What are those?

"Rats?" I cried out.

Deirdre looked up at me and frowned. Her eyes welled up. "I found them in a dumpster. Their mamma was dead. Poison. Luckily I got there before any of these little fellows drank from her teat; otherwise they would have died too." She held them up to me. "Katrina, meet Captain Excellent, Hannibal King and Van Wilder."

"Captain Excellent, Hannibal King and ... let me guess, those are all characters Ryan Reynolds has played?"

Deirdre was obsessed with Ryan Reynolds. More than obsessed. Absolutely in love with him. I'd already had more than a few nightmares about bailing her out of jail on stalking charges. But then again, given how absolutely beautiful Deirdre was, it might not ever make it to trial.

Deirdre confirmed my guess with a nod. "Yes ... Ryan is the best," she said in a dreamy voice as she held three toy baby bottles between her fingers and fed them what I hoped was milk ... as in, *from a cow.* You never know what lengths a changeling would go through to accommodate an animal in need, and I wouldn't put it past her to find some mamma rat and "borrow" its milk. Or try to make her own.

"You can't keep them," I said, knowing full well that I was inviting a conversation about rules and regulations, and how some humans were adverse to rats, mice and just about any other type of rodent, especially when said rodent's previous home was a literal dumpster.

But instead of the usual conversation where I explained the way things worked in the GoneGod world, she simply nodded and said, "I know. As soon as I can, I shall release them into the forest and let them find their way."

The tears were suddenly back.

"There is so much that will eat them … I just want to give them a fighting chance to survive."

I ignored this, opting to plop myself down on my bed.

I got into bed and pulled out Egya's notes. Even though his handwriting was very neat—too neat, if you asked me. His handwriting made the paper look like some sacred text you'd find on a Dead Sea Scroll or ancient tomb's wall. I felt shame just touching it.

I don't know why Psychology 101 was giving me so much trouble. I suspect it was because I had spent so long *not* being a human, I was having trouble relating.

Egya liked to tell me my mental block on the subject stemmed from a fear that I'd get outed as not being human. I had spent the last four years hiding my vampiric past, and now I had to write about the human condition—and I was being graded for it. If I did it wrong enough, surely I'd get caught.

I could just imagine my prof holding my test, pointing at me and yelling, *"Not human! Not human!"* I'd had *that* nightmare plenty of times, too, which I'm sure could have been explained somewhere in Egya's notes on the human condition. Oh, the irony. I'm also sure these thoughts were just driven by my anxiety over failing. And I'm *extra* sure my thoughts about my thoughts were inspired by this class.

A vicious cycle, really.

I shook my head, driving out these distracting thoughts. All I needed was a C and I'd pass Psychology 101. Just a C. Then I'd never have to pretend to know what it's like to be human ever again.

I started to go through his notes and got about halfway down page one when the incessant sucking noise from the baby rats grated my brain.

"Can you *stop* that?"

Aggression as a response to anxiety—maybe I was human after all.

Deirdre looked up at me, confused, the movement causing the vines that had been draped over her various lady parts like an old Eve painting to move, and suddenly I was exposed to her … well, let me phrase it using a term from my era: *whispering eye.*

27

I shook my head, took a calming breath, averted my gaze and said, "Can you feed them anywhere else? I need to study."

"They're done anyway," she said, standing up, exposing all her glory—and let me tell you, Mother Nature gave her *tons* of glory—and put the mischief of pups in an aquarium filled with grass and other stuff she'd dug up from the forest behind our dorm. Then, gently tapping the glass wall, she said, "Poor guys, growing up without a mother."

I snorted. "They don't know how lucky they are."

Deirdre turned and gave me a curious look. "Why would you say that?"

I didn't answer. I had enough of talking about my mother for this century, let alone one day. Clearly Egya's Psych notes were making me vulnerable.

The changeling gave me an admonishing look—no small feat to accomplish when you were fully naked, but GoneGodDammit if Deirdre didn't pull it off—and said, "Don't speak so ill of mothers— they are the vines from which all life grows. They are the fountain which nourishes—"

"Yeah, yeah, yeah, Mother Nature's the tits—I get it, Deirdre, but can you spare me the lecture in which every other word has something to do with nature? I've really got to study."

And with that, I stuck my nose into my books—and failed to study.

Instead, my mind wandered to another time altogether.

4

THE PAST AND ALL THAT JAZZ

Old Scotland—The Day Before Katrina Darling's Death

No fulfilled birthday wishes for me. Instead, I was turned one fateful evening just after my fifteenth birthday. That evening there was a cèilidh in town—one of our old Scottish traditions, a gay old time with song and dance and stories—and I was determined to go.

My mother, of course, was determined I did not.

Her reasoning was this—young Gareth Classes, handsome and from a good upbringing, had his sights on me. And I, being fifteen and falsely convinced that I was a woman now, welcomed said sights with my flirtatious glances and coy smiles. My mother, being my mother, wasn't convinced: He was a bit too handsome, in her opinion, and he'd spoil me! His upbringing wasn't *that* good—she'd heard there was a half-cousin twice removed somewhere in the family tree who had a unibrow. "And that, as we all know," she'd say every chance she got, "is a sign of inbreeding."

I was not to go. My father was not to escort me, as would have been proper at the time. So, denied, my father's hands tied, I went sulking to my bedroom.

Or so I pretended. But I had already known that my mother wouldn't let me go, and had prepared. I was fifteen—I wasn't born yesterday! And so, pulling out my dress from beneath my bed, I climbed out my window and ran to the old birch behind the barn where I had tied up my horse (saddled and all—wasn't born yesterday, remember?).

Before riding off, I tipped the new farm hand my father had hired not to tattle on me. The young man nodded, grateful for the extra coin.

I knew my mother would leave me to my mourning till morning, letting me cool off before engaging me again. That was her pattern, and she never broke her patterns, so I was fairly sure that I would get away with it.

And if not? Well, I was willing to suffer the consequences of being caught. Gareth was waiting.

Once at the dance, I quickly dressed and joined the festivities. My dance card filled up upon arrival—not that I was all that popular with the lads, but Gareth's name managed to find its way to almost every slot.

We danced the Gypsy Thread, Strip the Willow and Duke of Perth, Knot on a Ferry, Fairy Ring and White Sergeant (not as racist as you might think—at the time, pretty much every sergeant in Scotland was as white as curdled milk).

And when the cèilidh ended, Gareth—handsome and of good upbringing—offered to escort me home. Gentleman that he was. And lady that I was, I accepted graciously. We both had the same gleam in our eyes, but, hey, we kept that from the others. My first engagement in foreplay, in a weird way.

We rode up halfway, before stopping near the loch and beginning to commence in the very activity my mother had tried to protect me from.

It was a brisk night, but desire and teenage foolery kept me warm. It was also a full moon, which meant there was just enough light to illuminate his face (did I mention it was handsome?), but not enough to warn us as a dark figure approached, moving far too silent for what the landscape suggested possible.

Gareth was gently kissing my neck when he was ripped off, his body tossed ten meters away from me as if one were discarding a sack of potatoes. I did not know it at the time, but Gareth died before he hit the ground.

And then the monster—the monster that had, ironically, saved my maidenhood—climbed on top of me, replacing Gareth's gentle kissing with fangs and pain.

I don't know how long the monster drained me. I was lost in the moment of dying—it was painful, yes, but it was also sensual in a way I couldn't explain, which, I suppose, was something my mother had been trying to protect me from too.

But I was not so lost in that moment that I didn't feel something heavy strike the monster above me.

The vampire—I'm sure you guessed it was a vampire—released me and turned to face whoever had hit him, and that is when I saw my father standing there, an axe in one hand, his dirk in the other.

I guess Mother didn't wait till morning, after all.

I did not see what happened after that, only learning later that my father attacked the vampire with all he had, and although he did not manage to kill the creature, he did manage to chase him off.

My father had saved me. Or so he thought.

↔

The next morning I woke up in my own bed. My body felt heavy, sluggish, difficult to move. It was as if I was buried under a thousand blankets—which I wasn't. I was far too feverish for my cotton night-dress, let alone a blanket. Unencumbered, it felt as though my blood had been replaced with liquid lead.

Later—after I sired my first acolytes—I learned how right I was. When your body begins to take on the vampire virus, your blood becomes turgid—think molasses. And very heavy—think molasses trying to flow uphill. Movement is difficult because you are literally being weighed down by your insides—think molasses trying to … well, you get the idea.

But I wouldn't learn what it was like for molasses to try to flow uphill for some time. At that moment all I knew was that I couldn't move, I felt immense pain unlike anything I had ever known and my mother was by my side, dabbing my forehead with cool water she must have gathered from the nearby brook.

I could hear her cloth dip into the bucket and then the gentle drip as she wrung out the excess water back into the bucket. A gentle dab, dab, dab until my fever eventually turned the cold cloth into something hot and unpleasant to touch. Every time she placed the hot cloth back into the water, I could hear her suck air through the slight gap between her two front teeth.

She did that every time she was nervous.

Dab, dab, dab. Slosh. Suck.

Dab, dab, dab. Slosh. Suck.

I don't know how long that went on for—hours, days, weeks.

It wasn't as if time had stopped. I could still sense the seconds marching painfully on. But where those seconds would lead—at the time I had no idea. Had I known, I might have done whatever was left in my diminishing power to stop their progression altogether.

↔

The morning I regained consciousness and some semblance of movement, I awoke to Mother sleeping on the chair next to me, and Father standing by the open window.

"Fa—" I started, but my voice caught in my throat.

My father turned around, his eyes widening, and I knew from the glistening tears jerking from his eyes that my waking was a great surprise to him. He had been preparing to say goodbye—to bury his daughter. And now that I was awake, he could hope that a headstone would no longer be necessary.

He was half-right.

"Don't speak," he said, darting to my side. He poured some water in a cup and helped me sip it. "Here, drink this."

I felt the rim of the cold cup on my lips and longed for the relief that the cool water dripping down my throat would bring. But it did not sooth me or quench my thirst. Rather, it felt like someone was pouring gritty, caustic sand into my throat.

I coughed and pushed the water away from me.

"How long?" I managed, but my father didn't need to answer for me to know. I estimated at least ten days based on the light bruise marks on my father's face. The prizes of his fight with my predator. He must have put up one hell of fight to chase away a vampire, and taken many blows in the process—regardless of the fact that he was lucky to still be alive. But he was basically healed now, his face baring light yellow marks as evidence of what he did.

For me.

"Ten days, my little angel, my beautiful cherub," he said.

Cherub—that's what he called me whenever he was proud or happy, worried or angry. Come to think of it, that's what he always called me.

I swallowed and coughed again. "And Gareth?"

In answer, he held up his hands and showed me the dirt beneath his nails.

That was when I first noticed my heart had stilled. "When?"

"Yesterday," he said. "It was a beautiful ceremony. I wish you could have been there to say goodbye."

"I as well, Father."

"Are you in pain?" he asked.

I started to say yes, but examining myself, I found that the heaviness had left me, as had the pain. I still ached, but that stemmed more from thirst and hunger. My actual body felt whole. Strong, even.

I shook my head.

My father gave me a strange, worried look—the first of many. He had expected me to say that I still hurt, that I was still suffering, but no pain? That was cause for concern.

"I'll go get the doctor," he said.

"No, Father. Please," I said, reaching for his hand. "Stay. Just a little longer."

He gave me a pleasant smile and nodded. He placed a gentle hand on my mother's arm, said, "Look who is awake."

My mother—for that was who she was when she was human—stood up and, nearly falling on me, gave me the most uncomfortable, painful and wonderful hug of my life.

"Darling—you had us so worried. So terribly, terribly worried."

My father, crying now in earnest, nodded and hugged me too.

Had I known that would be the last time the three of us would embrace as a family, I would have held on longer.

Hell—I would have never let go.

5

DIN, DIN TIME

resent Day—

Of course, that was all then and this was now. And now demanded that I get ready for dinner. Harsh, sure, but I'd had a long time to bury my emotions surrounding that fateful day. And I was still a teenager, which meant when I was hungry, I was *hungry*. I guess in that way, not much had changed from my vampire days to now.

I went over to my closet and tried to pick an outfit that would both impress my mother and be un-criticize-able, if such a thing were possible. Nothing too low cut, nothing too far above the knee. Something that was both modern and classic. I thought about how she dressed, with the gaudy purple skirt and blazer that hugged her body.

Then I thought about the hair bun and oversized glasses. She was going for an updated 1960s look, and I had to admit—to myself, I'd never say it out loud ... on purpose, that is—she pulled it off.

Fine, if she was going for updated 1960s, I'd do her one better and hit the '70s. Not the hippie look, mind you. I hated the bell-bottoms and tie-dye shirts, the I'm-Earthy look, which was really just an excuse to be messy and unkempt. Take a shower, ya know?

I'd go for the professional 1970s woman. Chinos with wide bottoms (not quite bell-bottoms, thank the GoneGods, but wide enough that the pants didn't hug my calves), a colorful thick-striped tight-fitting long-sleeve shirt, bright yellow socks and red, low-heeled shoes.

Pulling out my Merino-wool plaid scarf, I looked at myself in the mirror. My colorful outfit matched and, what's more, I was a full decade ahead of my mother.

This would have to do.

As I dressed, Deirdre was attending to her pups—which were not to be confused with cute baby dogs, but rather disgusting new-born rats. She hardly looked up at me as I dressed, which was strange. Normally my outfits fascinated the changeling, inspiring her to ask me a million questions about matching colors or styles or whatever ran through that changeling's head. (If she had it her way, we'd all be naked, all the time.)

But today, she was distant, more concerned with the lives of her rats than anything else. Thank the GoneGods.

When I was ready, I turned to my fae roommate and said, "I'm off."

Deirdre didn't look up, just giving me an absent wave goodbye.

Something was wrong—but I didn't have time to figure out what it was now.

Maybe tomorrow. Hopefully those rats would be on their own "path" by then.

↔

Mama's Diner stood across from an old abandoned theatre that students tried to revive about once a year. Trouble with the theatre was that it was too big to be practical—some overly ambitious rich benefactor, surely—and the renovations too great to be done on the cheap. So the various attempts always fell apart before they really got started—which was particularly annoying, because the movie advertised was *Jaws*. No one even bothered to change that. A bit ironic, really—I dress as a woman from the '70s and here I am, scoffing at that decade's greatest achievement in film. Sorry, Spielberg.

I got to Mama's Diner early and saw that I was the second to arrive. I had hoped that Justin would have been there so we could talk —and kiss—but of course my hunky boyfriend wasn't early. He'd be fashionably late just so he could make an entrance. What a diva.

No, the other person there was Egya, standing with two bouquets of flowers in his hands. One an assortment of lilies, the other yellow roses.

"For you," he said, handing me the lilies.

I raised an eyebrow. "And the other one?"

"Who else? Justin, of course," he said with a wide-rimmed smile.

"Of course," I echoed, returning his smile. Thing about Egya—he may be a pain-in-the-ass ex-werehyena who generally got his kicks from riling you up, but his smile was infectious. To *not* smile back was akin to not taking in a whiff of freshly baked apple pie.

And I love apple pie.

"So …" he started, "your mom's in town."

"You don't say," I said, eyes wide in mock shock.

"How you feeling about that?"

"Look, if this is some setup for a joke or some snide comment, I'm really not in the—"

He touched my hand and positioned himself so that he was in front of me. Then, luring me in with eyes as dark as a black hole, he said, "No—really. How are you doing?"

I blinked my way out of the black hole. "I'm OK."

"Come on, Katrina. Don't bullshit me."

I pulled my hand away. "What do you want? I'm OK. Thanks for the flowers."

"What is the shortest distance between two points?"

"Excuse me?"

"You heard me ... what is the shortest distance between two points?"

"I don't know, Egya. A straight line?" I said, doing my best to *not* hide my irritation.

He smiled. "The truth."

"Ha-ha," I said.

"It's not a joke, girl. Now tell me ... how are you doing? Really?"

I scanned his face for a hint of humor, some pending joke preparing to pounce, and saw none. He was genuinely concerned. Egya could be amazing when he wanted to be. Which was once in a blue moon. (Werehyena pun intended.)

Shaking my head, I said, "I don't know. She's acting ... strange."

"How so?"

"Like a mom. She hasn't behaved like that since she was ... you know."

"Human?"

I nodded.

"Not so strange, then—she's human now."

"I guess. But you know what it was like to lose our, ahhh, Other-half. It wasn't like our personalities just reverted back to our human days too."

"True, but being only human is still different—from what we were, at least—and that can have a profound effect on people."

"I suppose. Still ..." I shook my head again, biting my lower lip. "But she's not just here for me. So there's clearly still a bit of the Queen Bitch in her. Seems my mother is working for—"

"Yoohoo!" I heard my mother's voice call from down the street.

I had expected her to be walking, but instead found that she was sitting in the passenger seat of an old Mustang Convertible ...

Next to my boyfriend.

Stylishly late, as always.

↔

. . .

"Look who I found walking here," Justin said, pulling up the car next to us.

I stared down at my mother, who had substituted her purple suit for casual jeans and a low, white silk blouse that not only showed off her substantial cleavage, but also the scallop-wide, strap lace of her bra.

So much for going classy, Mother, I thought.

"Pish-posh, darling," my mother said. "There is nothing classier than an older woman embracing her femininity." Then, as if I couldn't be more horrified, she scooped up her ... ahem, *girls* ... jiggling them a bit, and drawing the eyes of both Egya and my boyfriend in the process.

"Mooom," I said, feeling like an embarrassed teenager again.

"Lighten up, darling. I'm human, too," she said, popping out of the car. Once outside, she pretended to curtsey (in jeans, classy) and said, "Thank you, young man, for rescuing a wandering soul from the side of the road."

Egya handed my mother the second bouquet, which I now saw was actually made of chrysanthemums, Black-eyed Susans, yellow roses, peonies and a sunflower as its centerpiece. "In the Taoist tradition, the golden flower—symbolized by this bouquet of yellow flowers—symbolizes the highest enlightenment. And given that you are sure to enlighten us with embarrassing stories about Katrina as a child, it was an easy choice." He sent a gleaming smile my way as he extended his arm to my mother and said, "Shall we?"

Show-off ... no-good ... charmer.

I waited for Justin to park his car so that I could give him a practiced glare. "Just found her on the street, huh?"

"Yeah," he said, sensing he might have done something wrong. "She really was on the side of the road."

"I didn't realize you were in the habit of picking up streetwalkers."

He gulped. "She's your mom."

"And?" I knew I was being difficult and didn't care.

39

"I'm going to go with 'sorry.' Not sure *why* I'm sorry, but I do know that I am very, very, very sorry," he said. "Add as many very's as you need, and I'll double them with kisses."

I guess Egya isn't the only charmer.

"Good." I gestured for him to extend his arm—which he did. "Now escort me inside, please."

↔

Egya and Mother already had drinks in front of them—and, I noticed, Mother's was half empty. (Or half full?)

Egya pushed out a seat for me. I was positioned so that I could see the door, which is how I liked it. As a vampire, I got into the habit of always facing a door—that way I could see who was entering and be on the lookout for any anti-vampire people. Didn't happen often, since it was rare that I'd manage to be officially invited inside a building, but old habits die hard. Besides, you never knew when you'd run into your estranged father and his Divine Cherubs.

Not that I had to worry about that anymore.

Still, it was nice of Egya to save me that seat, a safe distance from my mother. I'd have to add "considerate" in the column that off-set all the ticks in the "annoying" column.

"So, what is everyone having?" I asked, looking at the menu.

"Darling, according to this tall, dark and handsome gentleman, one must order poutine."

"You know what poutine is, don't you, Mother? Or did that tall, dark and whatever neglect to tell you?"

"I know what I *thought* it was," she said with a wink.

At this Egya howled with real, genuine laughter that took an awkward amount of time to wind down to a few last chuckles. Seems it wasn't only his smile that was infectious. Justin started snickering before letting out a full roar of laughter.

40

A couple seconds later, we were all laughing.

Between chuckles, I looked over at my mother, who was dabbing away tears of joy, and thought, *Maybe being human does change you.* I allowed myself to relax. *This dinner is going way better than expected*, I thought.

"Of course, darling, what did you expect to happen?"

Damn out-loud me! I shrugged and said, "What always happens with us? Arguments, fights, often explosions."

And as if the GoneGods were listening in on our conversation, the glass wall behind me shattered in an explosion of tiny dagger-like shards and three beings in black-ops uniforms and cherub masks came crashing through.

Whatever happened to using the door?

PART II
INTERMISSION

EARLIER—

George and Ringo had been in position to nab the vampire bitch as soon as she left the hotel, just like they planned. There's an alleyway about fifty yards away from the hotel's front door—perfect place to grab her. But then some college idiot pulled up in his old Mustang and —well, so much for their plan.

What is that expression? *We make plans and God laughs.* Well, God and the gods are gone—so Simione wonders if anyone is laughing now. He certainly isn't.

"Abort," Simione says in the walkie-talkie. "We'll get her later."

"Copy that," George says, and although Ringo's a good five feet away from the walkie-talkie, Simione still hears the kid groan.

"Don't worry, kid—we'll get her. We'll get them both. Come on back to the van and we'll figure out next steps."

Ringo gave a thumbs-up.

The two brothers started trotting toward him. Ringo's real name is

Ryan, but given he's George's little brother and ugly as sin, the nickname Ringo's too fitting not to use. The kid's carrying the large duffle bag filled with all the goodies. Simione scans the street to make sure no cops are around. Two guys dressed in all black, with large conspicuous bags, screams up-to-no-good.

But that isn't the case. They're up to *good*. They're up to a hell of a lot of good.

They're hunting vampires.

↔

After the gods left and all the Others showed up, there were a lot of personal vendettas settled. Mostly between Others—but humans got into the game, too. Humans who were hurt by creatures of the night—werewolves, zombies … vampires.

Now that they weren't souped-up creatures anymore, they were vulnerable and a hell of lot easier to take down.

During the early days, you could kill an ex-vampire right in the middle of Times Square and as long you could prove that the guy bleeding on the street was, once-upon-a-time, a demon, the cops were more likely to give you a high five than read your Miranda rights.

Those were the golden days. Golden days that lasted about six months. Then the politicians and police got their shit together and they came up with some kind of amnesty program. A clean slate. A do-over. After all, the rules had changed and vampires weren't vampires no more—they were human.

"Well, fuck that!" Simione mutters as George and Ryan jump in the van.

"Fuck what?" George asks.

"I was just thinking how that bitch keeps getting lucky. We need to make her *unlucky*."

The two brothers nod, grinning. "What's the plan?" This from George—obviously.

"Stake out the hotel. Maybe we'll get lucky and she'll come back in the dead of night, drunk and ripe for the—" He draws a finger across his own throat.

George chuckles, but Ringo isn't laughing. He's got that deadly stare going for him. Like he can't wait to kill her. The boy's hungry. Good.

Putting a heavy hand on the silent kid's shoulder, Simione nods and says, "But let's grab some grub, first. Can't serve justice on an empty stomach. There's a diner not too far from here."

↔

They drive by the diner and lo-and-behold, the kid's Mustang is parked out front. Grub would have to be grabbed later.

Driving slowly past the place, they look in the window ... and Simione cannot believe what he sees. Not only is that middle-aged vampire bitch sitting there, but so is her daughter.

"Katrina," he mutters to himself.

"What'd you say?" George asks.

Simione ignores George, staring at little miss Katrina Darling with her lush auburn hair and million-dollar smile. She looks so good, so innocent. So harmless. But Simione knows better. He knows who she *really* is ...

So we got us two targets, he thinks. *Time to plan, figure out a trap and determine the best course of action to take them down.*

But—like the old expression goes—humans plan and God laughs.

Except it isn't God laughing, Simione knows. It's Katrina and her bitch mom. *They're* laughing.

Laughing like they don't have a care in the world.

Simione's idea for plans and traps and courses of action goes out the window.

"Suit up, boys," he says, gritting his teeth. "Time to take these bitches down."

6

WHEN AN ANGEL SHATTERS A WINDOW, USE THE DOOR

*W*hen my father started the Divine Cherubs, what most believed his mission statement to mean was that humans were taking the role of angels on Earth and hunting the nasty things that go bump in the night.

Few knew that what he actually meant was they were to hunt *me*—his little "cherub." At first I was hurt that he'd use my nickname against me. Every time I heard that a Divine Cherub was in town or saw one of those child-like masks, my heart would flutter with a combination of fear and despair.

I'd also wonder if one of the men beneath the mask was my father.

But then my father died and his Divine Cherubs charged on without him throughout the centuries, fortunately unorganized and more of an old boys' club than anything to be taken seriously.

I hadn't seen one in decades. After the GrandExodus, I hadn't expected to encounter one again.

Now I was human, sitting in a diner near my university, and the last thing I expected was to see a Divine Cherub—and certainly not one of the organization's legendary Hunters.

Let alone *three*.

↔

They came crashing through the window and my old instinct flooded into me. This was a life-or-death scenario that I had played out many times before and I immediately got up to meet their attack, completely forgetting that I was a human.

With the adrenaline flowing and my temporary amnesia, I half-expected my vampire strength to kick in. I targeted their leader—the biggest guy at the front—meaning to throw him back out of the window they came crashing through. But instead of easily repelling them like I had done for centuries, my arms met stone.

I mean, *actual stone*. Either this guy was a freaking gargoyle or he was wearing something underneath his black, button-up shirt. He paused for a second, his crisp green eyes behind the mask meeting mine. The corners of his eyes crinkled, and I guessed he was smiling.

Then he grabbed my two wrists, twisted with unnatural strength, and threw me against one of Mama's unshattered walls. I crashed into the decorative plates Mama (or whoever owned this place) hung on the walls with a thud.

Both Egya and Justin were up in a flash. Justin, being nineteen and never having the benefit of once being vampire or werewolf, sought to meet the smallest of the three head on. Strength against strength … and the poor guy didn't stand a chance. His adversary simply put a hand on his chest and pushed, sending Justin flying toward the kitchen in the back.

Egya, on the other hand, had centuries of experience. Seeing how strong these guys were, he opted not to attack head-on. Instead, he got close and then dropped to his knees, using the freshly waxed floors to slide past his attacker.

Once behind him, he grabbed one of the tables and smashed it into the guy's back. Human or not, Egya was strong. As were the tables—they were commercial beasts designed to endure endless parades of customers, waiters and bussers. Heavy and well-made.

Getting hit by one of those in the back was the equivalent of getting hit by a wall.

But the guy must not have gotten the memo—he took it like it was nothing, turning around and pushing Egya out the front door.

Justin and Egya out of the picture, the biggest guy turned on me, yelling to his cronies, "Get the other bitch!"

"She's gone," said the smallest of the three.

"What do you mean, *gone*?" he said, scanning the diner.

Yeah, what do you mean, "gone"? I scanned the diner too, and sure enough there was not a trace of my good ol' mom. I guess she wasn't that different after all … always running away when things got too hot, daughter be damned.

But just when my judgmental rage was reaching full throttle, I heard my mother yell, "Darling—to me!" Then she threw a motherf-reaking meat cleaver at the guy closest to me.

She was in the kitchen, hand reached out in my direction. I didn't need to be told twice. Miracles happen every day—why gawk at one when it's handed to you? I jumped to my feet, over the counter and through the window where my mother's arms were there to help me through.

Once I was inside, she threw something I didn't quite see, followed by a bottle of whisky stuffed with a cloth already on fire. The thing exploded like a fireball, creating a pool of fire between us and the three hunters.

"What a waste of whisky," she said. "This way."

"What about Justin?"

"He's already outside."

"And Egya?"

She groaned in frustration and grabbed my wrist. "I see your habit of always doubting your mother hasn't changed," she groaned as she pulled out back.

Outside, I saw Egya grinning in the driver's seat of Justin's Mustang, Justin in the back, clearly dazed from the attack.

He looked at me with glazed eyes. "What the—?"

"Your mother is one fast-thinking lady," Egya said, leaning over and opening the passenger's side door. "She threw me the keys just before she threw the Molotov cocktail."

So that was what she threw. Keys. I had to admit—kind of badass.

"Come on, girl. We gotta ride!"

I jumped into the backseat, my mother the passenger seat.

Once inside, Egya cried out, "Shadowfax—show me the meaning of haste!" and slammed on the accelerator.

What a dork.

7

MUSTANGS, CONFUSED BOYFRIENDS AND LAUGHING HYENAS

*E*gya drove the Mustang away from the diner and it took all of seven seconds for the guy who understood the least about what was going on to break the silence.

"What the friggin' … effing … *fuck* was that?" Justin cried out, his eyes wide with fear.

"Language, dear, I am your elder—and from the way you two look at each other, a potential mother-in-law."

At this Justin blushed, before repeating in a far more controlled tone, "What just, erm … happened?"

"We were attacked, dear."

"Mother, stop calling him 'dear,' " I said.

"Your wish is my command, darling." She turned back to Justin. "Honey, those men were—"

"They were after money or something—they clearly were after something," I cut in. "Just your average, everyday robber."

Smooth, girl, real smooth!

My mother was no idiot. She got it immediately that I didn't want my three-hundred-year-old secret out of the bag—the secret that I had major daddy issues. She gave me a sly wink and said, "The way they move, I suspect they were there to shut Mama's down."

"Mama's?"

"Yes, honey—isn't that the name of the diner? Clearly whoever owns Mama's is connected."

"Connected?" Justin repeated, his voice skeptical.

"I've seen it before. Mob flare-ups—fights, going to the mattresses, that kind of stuff."

"And you've seen it before?" Justin asked.

Sure, on The Wire, Sopranos, The Godfather, *all the classics,* I thought.

Egya howled at this, but both Justin and my mother gave me a blank look.

"Darling, I know things. I've told you before. I am employed by—"

"Mother ..." I said in a warning tone.

"My point is, I know things, and that had mafia beef written all over it." The way she said *beef* sounded so unnatural it was like a fish trying to roar out of water.

"But it doesn't make sense. For one thing, they came right at you," Justin said, looking at me. "And they were wearing your mask, and—"

My eyes widened at this and Justin immediately took the hint, shutting up—but it was too late. Shit.

A few weeks ago the dorms were attacked by a fanatical human who thought that if she sacrificed enough students and spilled enough innocent blood, she could please the gods enough into coming back. Egya, Deirdre, the Avatar of Truth—Mergen, sweet guy—and myself had successfully fought her off.

And I had been wearing my father's Cherub mask when doing so.

Almost no one knew about that except Justin, who had seen me put it on. And now he was blabbing about that in front of the absolute last person I wanted to know what had happened.

My mother had clearly heard him, and in a dry, humorless tone, she said, "Moonlighting as your father, I see."

I tried to ignore the comment, but knowing how my blemish-free cheeks work, I was sure I had turned bright pink. "Never mind that now," I mumbled.

Mention of my father confused the others. Justin's eyes met mine, open wide in confusion, and I tried my best to mentally project that I would tell him everything when we were alone. *Promise.*

He projected back that I better.

I had hoped I'd be able to keep my secret from him a bit longer—like sixty or seventy years. You know, death-bed confessions and all. But that was a luxury I could no longer hope for. Not if I wanted to keep him. Now I could only hope that when I did tell him, he'd still want to be with me.

"We should call the police," Justin finally said.

"Already done," my mother said, wiggling her cellphone.

"What? When?" I asked.

She shrugged, seemingly unconcerned. "Sometime between pulling Justin out the back door and setting the place on fire, I believe?"

We fell into an awkward silence that was momentarily broken by Egya saying, "So ... anyone still hungry?"

When no one laughed, he grunted and joined us in our uncomfortable hush.

I was painfully aware of Justin's eyes on me. He wasn't going to let this "father" stuff rest for long. Boy, did I miss the days when I could hypnotize humans, or I had the strength to simply knock them out. But continuing to keep Justin in the dark was a no-go—neither was dropping him off at home with those Cherub maniacs on the loose.

"Well," I said, unable to take the quiet anymore, "we can't just drive around aimlessly. We need somewhere we can think. And talk."

Egya snapped his fingers and said, giggling, "I have just the place," as he turned on a winding road that led up the hill.

↔

McGill University and the city that houses it are built on a hill. Well, technically it's a volcano so dead that even the gods couldn't get it to burp before they packed up and booked it. At the top of the hill stands a big neon cross that, despite the absence of the god it was built for, the city decided not to turn off. Tax dollars be damned. As a vampire —ex or not—crosses make me nervous, and yet I'd found myself basking under its neon glow more than once. Maybe I secretly figured it was the last place a Divine Cherub would come looking.

"Really? Here?" my mother said as soon as Egya's destination became clear. Then, believing that Justin and Egya didn't know that we were ex-vampires (although I could see a dawning realization in her eyes that Egya knew more than he should), she adopted a softer tone. "*Love* your innovative thinking. Both a safe haven and tourist spot. Bravo." She was trying to spin as much levity in her tone as she could, but we all could sense the stress in her voice.

Once at the cross, I jumped out of the car and waited impatiently for Justin to get out. The second his feet touched the asphalt, I grabbed his hand and pulled him into the brush.

"Darling," my mother called out, "this is hardly the time for a snog. The Quad's nowhere near here!"

I know it wasn't right, her being my mom and all, but I gave her the finger and pulled him deeper into the tree line until I was sure no one could hear us. She'd done worse to me, trust me.

Before I could say anything, he bent down and kissed me. "You OK?" he asked.

That's Justin—always says the right thing in a shitstorm of wrong.

"I'm OK," I said. "Are you?"

He kissed me again. "Of course. What else did you expect?"

"I don't know. For you to be more human. Yelling, maybe a good 'What the hell is going on?,' perhaps a 'What are you keeping from me?' "

He nodded. "So … what *are* you keeping from me?"

"I can't tell you."

"Can't or won't?" He stared at me like he was trying to drown me in his ocean-blue eyes. "I know that you're not an ordinary girl, Kat, just like I know that was no mafia attack. Those guys wore your mask. They were gunning for *you*, not the diner. Who are they? Former members of your"—he paused, thinking of the word—"gang? Humph —maybe your mom was right."

I chuckled. "She's a fantastic liar … and her lies always have just enough truth to keep you from knowing the *truth*-truth."

Justin nodded, but he still looked confused. "And the truth is …?"

"First of all—not a gang, more like a clan. Scottish, remember? Secondly, they're not the ex-members—I am. Well … sort of. And lastly, I don't—"

"I know, you don't want to tell me."

"I *do*, just in the right way. It's so complicated, and in this rushed, intense situation, I'll say the wrong thing and—"

He kissed me. Hard.

I pulled away. "And you'll—"

Another kiss.

"—never speak to me again."

He kissed me again, pausing to say, "Who said anything about speaking?"

↔

I convinced Justin to let Egya, my mother and me speak in private. I could see that he was hurt that Egya was privy to information he wasn't, but he also understood enough to know that the reason Egya knew more than he did was because we weren't an item. Justin and I were. And in a strange way, that meant I had to protect him from that information. For now, at least.

So he nodded, getting into the driver's seat of his car and waiting for us to finish our palaver.

My mother's laughter broke into my apparently spoken-aloud thoughts. "Palaver, darling? Your speech always gets so archaic when you're stressed."

I ignored her dig at me and looked over at Egya who, surprisingly, said nothing. He didn't even laugh.

"So he knows?" my mother asked.

Egya nodded. "If by *he* you mean me, and by *knows*, you mean know that you and your daughter both had fangs once-upon-a-time, then yes."

"And did *you* have fangs? Once-upon-a-time?" my mother asked, lifting an eyebrow.

"Indeed, I did. Hyena." He lifted a hand like he was at an AA meeting.

"Vampire," my mother said, lifting her hand in the same manner.

When I didn't lift mine, she said, "You must learn to play more, darling."

"Divine Cherubs tried to kill us, Mom. Vampire hunters."

"Exactly—perfect time to laugh. Weren't those masks *silly?*"

I closed my eyes tight and counted to three. Out loud. Once calm, I said, "We're human now. What about the amnesty program?"

"You know what that group was like—they love their oaths and grudges. I suspect that they are of the variety that don't give a damn about amnesty."

"They're not human, that's for sure."

Egya and my mother gave me a confused look.

"How do you know?" Egya asked.

I returned their looks with one of my own. "Did you see them? They were far too strong. The big guy threw me like I was a stack of newspapers. No human—no matter how strong or well-trained— could do that so easily."

"Hate to break it to you, but you barely weigh as much as a stack of newspapers," Egya said. "Maybe a lightly packed knapsack."

"First of all, thank you, but we all know that's not true. I may be light, but I'm not *that* light. Also, I'm well-trained. I know how to manipulate my body to work against a throw, and he cut through my defenses without exerting anything remotely resembling effort. No, he was an Other—and one that knew what he was doing, too."

Egya nodded. "If you say so, then it is so."

Now who's guilty of archaic speech?

"Tell me, Mother, are they the 'danger' you warned me about?"

Egya looked at Charlie. "Danger? I thought you were just visiting, not bringing *danger* with you."

"I *am* visiting," my mother said in a faux defensive tone. "But can't a girl do both? And to answer your question, darling, no—these guys are not the danger I was warned about. They are far too unorganized. Laughable, really. You call that danger? The danger I meant comes from a far more formidable foe. One interested in the … you know, what we talked about."

Egya rolled his eyes. "I think we're beyond secrets."

"We are," I said. "My mother dearest is here because she is looking for—"

"Darling …" she said in a cautioning tone.

"Egya is my friend," I said. "And someone I trust with my life."

"Remember what we discussed. The wrong kind of knowing can change a person. Are you absolutely sure he will not change when presented with the possibility of the knowledge I seek?"

"Possibility, knowledge, change … can we play Twenty Questions? I'm an awesome guesser," Egya said. His tone was mirthful, but his narrowed gaze and pursed lips were not. He wanted answers.

I looked over at Egya, contemplating what my mother said. Would the desire to know where the gods went and why be too great a temptation for Egya to ignore? I wasn't sure. But then my gaze was drawn to the Mustang in the clearing and the young man who sat patiently for us to finish our palaver. He was sitting there, in the dark literally and metaphorically, and it was killing our relationship.

Enough secrets, I thought, this time in my head, and before my mother could stop me, I said, "She's looking for an amulet that supposedly knows where the GoneGods are."

"Ah … I see," was all Egya said.

↔

. . .

If Egya was desperate to possess such knowledge, neither his words nor expression betrayed it. He simply looked at me and asked skeptically, "You have such a talisman?"

"I don't ... but the Other Studies Library's museum section just might."

"I see," he said. "And those men. With the Cherub masks?"

Mother cut in. "My best guess? Coincidence. They're hunting me or darling, here. Ships in the night and all that jazz."

"Ships in the night miss each other—they don't crash into one another."

"Is that so, darling? Is that what they're teaching you at this school? I can never keep up with all these human expressions."

"You mean *your* expressions, Mother? Given you are human now?"

She waved a dismissive hand and said, "My point is that, as best I can tell, their attack and my quest are unrelated."

Egya said, "So ... what now?"

But I wasn't ready to change the subject. "The men. Were they attacking you or me, Mother?"

"Me, darling, me."

"How do you know?" I asked.

My mother gave me that look she always did when I missed something obvious or was being dense. A look that could send me from zero to sixty on the rage meter in half a second flat. I closed my eyes again and said through gritted teeth, "How, Mother Dearest, dost thou knowest thine claim?"

"Because, darling dearest," she hissed back, "they never bothered you until the day I showed up."

She had a point. *GoneGodDammit.*

"Swearing, darling."

"OK—so they're after you. Then the sooner you leave, the sooner they do too."

"So endearing how concerned you are for my safety, darling. Just warms a mother's heart."

I gave her a blank stare. I wasn't going to rise to her bait anymore.

"Very well—for the good of all, Mother must leave. That is my cross to bear." She looked up at the actual cross and put her palms together in pretend reverence.

"So what's the plan?" Egya asked, his smirk that of a man clearly amused by the theatre he's watching.

"Divine Cherubs, Other or not, do not hurt civilians," Mother said. "Justin and you are safe, so darling and I will get the amulet and—"

"I don't know about that not-hurting-civilians part. They weren't holding back despite us being with bloodbaits."

Egya gave me a look. "Bloodbaits?"

"Sorry, nickname. Means non-vampires."

He nodded, then, when he realized what it implied, his expression seemed torn between laughter and offense.

I turned back to my mother. "So?"

She shook her head, tisk-tisking. "Darling, darling … always looking out for everyone but herself."

I took a step toward my mother. "If you don't back the f—"

Egya stepped between us. "Modified plan. You two get the amulet, and I will go with Justin. If we're safe, then we have nothing to worry about. And if we're not safe—I might be human, but I haven't lost all of what I once was."

The ex-werehyena gave us such a wicked grin, sickly green under the neon glow of a giant cross, that the hairs on the back of my neck stood up.

8

GOODBYES, AMULETS

*J*ustin dropped mother and me off at the library, giving my hand a light squeeze in lieu of a kiss goodbye. I wasn't sure if it was in deference to my mother or a small protest for still being left in the dark. Egya, the cheeky bastard, kissed the back of my mother's hand. Then he gave me a high-five with such dorky vigor, I couldn't help but laugh. The two of them rode off into the night, away from us and hopefully toward safety.

"So, darling," my mother said, turning to the very closed and locked library door, "I don't suppose you have a key?"

↔

Several weeks ago my friend (David Dewey, but I'd always know him as the "Old Librarian") was murdered inside the Other Studies Library —the same friend whose late-delivered letter gave me just seconds' notice of my mother's arrival—and if I had only gotten there a few minutes earlier, I might have been able to save him. Add that to my list of nightmares.

Part of the reason why I couldn't get to him in time was because I had been locked out of the damn building. My solution had been to break the thick, stained-glass paneling that outlined the oak door.

After that I vowed I'd never be locked out again—and in the middle of the night (and with Egya's help)—we carefully removed the paneling as a secret entrance. Egya was good with his hands, and if I hadn't known where the two latches were, there was no way I'd get in. But I did and, carefully pulling them, I removed the paneling and shimmied inside. Given that the entrance was only about ten inches wide, I had to hold my breath. Definitely something I could do, especially with a sports bra (which I didn't have on now, but still managed, anyway; girl problems persisted even after three hundred years).

My mother, on the other hand, could have the greatest sports bra ever created and still her ample bosom would be too much for such a narrow passage.

I knew that—and still let her struggle before snapping my finger and saying, as if it were an afterthought, "I can unlock the door from the inside."

She glared at me, the side of one breast pressing no doubt painfully against the door. "Really, darling, we're stooping to *this* level of passive aggression?"

Indeed, we are, Mother. Indeed, we are.

↔

As I held the old oak door open for mother, I started to wonder for the first time why I was being so hard on her. I mean, outside of it being funny watching her try to get that hour-glass-shaped body of hers through a crack in the wall. Still, I was being hard on her for no real reason, wasn't I? So far everything she was doing seemed to be on the up-and-up. She'd been (relatively) nice, helped save Justin, got us out of a bind ...

Was I being a bad daughter?

Despite all that, my Spidey-senses were going nuts. (And before you ask—I don't actually have a Spidey-sense or any kind of preternatural warning system. I'm just a girl, standing in front of her mother, doubting every word, action and intention ... you know, normal family stuff.)

Once inside, I disabled the alarm. Not that it was much of an alarm —this ancient building has too many creeks and groans; a state-of-the-art alarm system would go off every thirty seconds. Or maybe that was just what the school board said to avoid the cost. This alarm was more of the for-show-only variety, which was strange given how valuable the artifacts in the museum were.

I accounted the lack of security to be chalked up to three things: one—humans still haven't grasped the power of magic and talismans imbued with magic; two—items identified as truly powerful were sent to maximum security facilities; and, finally, three—the powers that be realized that if an Other with either their superior strength or a willingness to burn a bit of time would break in here no matter how much security the library could install.

So in other words, this place lacked security because humans are ultimately cheap and lazy.

Hey—I get it. I'm one of them. Now.

My mother walked inside and scanned the old room. "So this is where you work now?" She sounded disappointed.

"Part-time job. Pays the bills. Keeps me busy."

"Darling, you have more money than sense. A perk of being alive longer than the bank system."

"Fine—then let's just go with 'keeps me busy.' "

"Justin should keep you busy enough."

I bit my tongue, not saying anything. I wasn't going to let her get to me.

"Unless he doesn't ..." she added, a hint of a question in her words.

Clamping down on tongue now.

"Which is a shame. A boy like him should be plenty enough. But if he isn't, he isn't."

Tongue has been severed clean off. Mouth bleeding profusely. Maybe if I'm lucky, I'll choke on my own blood.

"Perhaps you should consider that Egya fellow. He seems like he would be a jolly good time. Besides, him being an ex-were makes you two—"

I don't know why the mention of Egya set me off, but it did. I got in my mother's face and said, "What's the game here? I thought we were here for the amulet, not so you can give me dating advice."

"Can't a mother do both? Besides, you clearly need it."

I crossed my arms. "How do you figure?"

"Because I practically challenged Justin's manhood—and nothing. One little mention of Egya and"—she squeezed my cheeks—"all this."

Pushing away my mom's hands, I growled, "It's not Egya, Mother, it's *you*. Come on—let's get this damn amulet and get the hell out of here."

I'd let my mom touch a nerve, despite knowing to be on guard for just that. But the truth was, Justin and I were taking it slow. I liked to call it "1950s dating," because even though I lived (or *unlived?*) through the '50s I never got to enjoy the wholesome courting— sharing milkshakes, holding hands on the beach, going to Under the Sea–themed school dances, randomly breaking out into song and dance—the kind of stuff you saw in the old Elvis Presley movies.

I *know* dating in the '50s wasn't like the movies. People were just as horny then as they are now. But I liked the romantic idea of it—and Justin, to his immense credit, didn't seem to mind. Well, I'm sure he did mind … he's a boy, after all, with raging hormones. If he wasn't a little bit frustrated then there'd be something wrong with him, just like Mother implied.

Or something wrong with me.

OK, Kat, you're freaking yourself out. It's about doing this relationship right. Taking it slow. Because slow is safe.

But slow was a lie.

Late at night, when all the nightmare demons came knocking on my door, I knew what the truth was … and it's not that I liked the idea of a wholesome relationship worthy of a Norman Rockwell painting. The truth was I didn't want to get serious with Justin because I didn't want to tell him that I was a vampire, *ex-* or not.

↔

My mother had already confirmed that the amulet wasn't in any of the display cases in the Other Studies Library, so that left the archives.

The archives were situated in the basement level that, much like the first floor, was nothing but shelves and card catalogues. But unlike the first floor, very little of the cataloguing was actually on any computer database. Most of the stuff was still in boxes that weren't properly marked, the only tagging still in the original language of the donor. And since most donors were Others, that meant that most tags were still in elvish, orc, dracoon, wendigo and a whole host of other Other languages. Made me feel not so embarrassed about slipping into archaic English from time to time.

That was where I came in—my job was to modernize the whole operating system. A bit of a miss-hire, I know, since I was far from modern, but hey, at least I could read elvish (long story—let's just say I was briefly married to an elf prince before the Civil War, and he was a real asshole).

Seeing the task before us, my mother sighed. "Where do we start?"

"With whatever you can tell me about the damn thing."

↔

My mother's details were far too vague to be considered "details." She did know what it looked like—even provided me with a picture. What I saw was an inverted bulb with a wide neck. Within it was what looked like the Ancient Egyptian Key of Life … and something else.

"The Key of Life," I said. "That symbol has been tattooed on practically every hippie with an interest in mythology. The other symbol, however, is strange. It looks as if the bulb was trapping the key—"

"Or maybe the bulb represents the world's sky, which houses all life?" my mother offered, her voice betraying her excitement. I had never known my mother interested in the occult or symbols or anything other than enjoying the vampiric life and all it entailed. Maybe being human also leveled up your curiosity, too. It sure hadn't for me.

"OK—the sky. What cultures use that symbol for 'sky'?"

"I don't know, darling. That's more your thing than mine." She gestured vaguely toward the library surrounding us.

So her curiosity only goes so far, I thought.

"Far enough to risk my life for it," she said.

I clamped my lips shut, willing myself to stop with the out-loud narrative.

I turned the picture over, round and round. But I just didn't know, and my knowledge of semiotics was basic at best. The only reason I knew more than the average person was because I'd been around longer to see them. Key of Life and a, what? Sky, earth, trap? Which religions saw the sky as something that holds all life? The answer—all of them. But not all of them had practically built their entire dogma around it.

"Islam," I said, snapping my fingers. "They saw the night sky as being the emerald city—Qa—and given where its roots are, I could see early Islam sharing its symbology with Ancient Egypt."

My mother gave me a dubious look and for a moment I thought she was going to challenge my assessment. She didn't, thankfully. She just nodded and said, "So where is Islam and Ancient Egypt in all of this?"

↔

We must have gone through every box donated by jinn, jackal-guards, ifrits, nasnas and ghouls, but we turned up absolutely nothing. Not only did we not find the amulet, we didn't even find anything that remotely looked like the symbol. Sure there were plenty of papyruses with the Key of Life inscribed on them, but nothing with that bulbous symbol on it.

"There's nothing more you can give me other than this picture?" I asked in frustration.

My mother shook her head, tired. "All I have to go with is that it looks like that and it was donated to this museum."

"And how reliable are your sources?"

"Source," she corrected me. "And quite reliable."

I tilted my head. "How can you be so sure?"

"Because he's the donor," my mother said matter-of-factly.

I slapped my head on my forehead. "And he is ...?"

She blinked in confusion, waiting for me to finish. "He is ... what? I don't catch your meaning."

"Is he an Other?"

My mother shook her head. "*Was*, darling. He was. He's one of us."

"An ex-vamp?"

She cringed. "Darling—*vampire*. The shortened version of what we are is so ... base."

"*Were*, Mother," I fired back, mocking her tone. "We're not vampires anymore."

"You know my meaning. Anyway, he *is* an *ex*-vam*pire*. Dostarious, to be exact. Interesting fact about him ... he and his twin were turned at exactly the same time. Seems the Buities like the idea of turning twins. You know, they were born together, should die together and then rise together. Quite the sense of humor, the Buities—Andre and Adela. You remember them. He's a handsome Italian baron and she's ... well, she had the right kind of assets to keep him interested—"

I tuned my mother out as I looked up Dostarious's name, amazed that my mother simply didn't think of mentioning his name before—and frustrated that I hadn't thought to ask. My mother wasn't stupid. She omitted this little gem for a reason.

Damn. No Dostarious. He probably donated anonymously—most donors did not want anything tracing their donations back to them. Most magical items weren't very powerful, but they still had unusual effects, and Others—already distrusted—didn't want to be the ones responsible for accidently turning your cat into a frog. Or worse.

Which is all to say that Others were happy to get rid of their magical items—and to do so discretely. Dostarious seemed to not be an exception.

"Can you tell me anything about Dostarious?" I asked, interrupting her little monologue about the Buities.

"Dostarious? Only that he and his sister hate each other. Shame, really—in the fifteenth century they were the finest alchemists anywhere. It was said that even skinwalkers would go to them for help with their potions and—"

"Hold on," I interrupted, looking up. "What did you say?"

"Skinwalkers—you know, Native American Shamanic Others ... incredibly nasty, if you ask—"

"No, no—before that."

She paused. "They were the finest alchemists—"

"Of *course*," I said, standing up and slapping my forehead with the palm of my hand. I walked over to the reference books. "And you didn't think to tell me about Dostarious before?"

"This is your expertise, darling. It's not like you asked ..."

I have to give her that one.

"Thank you."

Dammit. Still, I thought, making sure it was firmly in my head, *my mother isn't stupid. She didn't tell me about the alchemist Dostarious for a reason. But given how obviously desperate she is to get the amulet, I can't figure out what the reason could possibly be ...*

I found the book I was looking for and flipped through it until I spotted the symbol. "That inverted bulb—it's not the sky, it's the alchemy symbol for …" I held out an image of an inverted jug (for lack of a better word) and showed it to my mother. It matched the symbol on the drawing. "Death. It's not the sky that is trapping the Key of Life … it's *death*."

"Interesting …" my mother said, and the tone of her voice said she was telling the truth.

"Interesting, indeed, Mother," I said, guiding her to the shelves that dealt with alchemy. Had to keep her looking while that interest was still piqued.

↔

Even though we had narrowed down our search, it still didn't mean that it was easy to find. It took forty-three boxes, a crap-load of sifting through oversized Ziploc bags and two papercuts—both mine—before we finally found the amulet.

Well, half of it, at least.

↔

"Shit, balls, shit, *shit*!" I growled.

"Language, darling."

"Fine—manure, testicles, scat, *poo*!"

"Darling—"

I threw the box I'd been holding onto the floor, not caring when its contents spilled. "Don't 'darling' me. We have exactly half an amulet, which means that I'm no closer to you leaving, am I?"

I shoved the amulet at my mother. It looked like the picture—if someone had ripped it in half. My mother looked at it, feeling its grooves along its edge where it had been torn from its twin half. "This is designed to be two pieces," she said, less as an observation and more like a statement that she'd already known.

I gave her my best what-aren't-you-telling-me look as I pulled the amulet out of her hands.

"I *knew* it was two pieces, darling. I just expected them to be together."

Something occurred to me, from when I was trying to tune her voice out. "You said they were twins?"

"Who?"

"Dostarious and whoever the other guy is ..."

"Girl. Or to use your modern twang: gal. Not all twins are identical."

"Do you think it's possible this *gal* has the other half?"

If my Psychology test was on the best display of passive-aggressive behavior, I'd ace the course.

"I suppose anything is possible. I will have to make enquiries." She reached into her purse and pulled out her cellphone. Then, sighing as if she just discovered that housekeeping didn't turn down her room, lifted the screen and said, "No signal."

9

NO SIGNALS FOR THE PAST

*W*e stepped outside so that my mother could call her "people"—whoever *they* were. The first rays of light were starting to shine—we had spent the night together in the Other Studies Library's archives. Not the first time we'd spent hours in a basement together—but if I was lucky, it would be the last.

Once outside, she tried to casually take the amulet from me—something I was definitely prepared for—but I held onto it to get a closer look and see if I could come up with any ideas as to what it was or how it worked. For something that was supposed to answer life's biggest question (in this GoneGod world, at least), you'd think it would have speakers or something. At the very least some instructions.

My brain was also itching at another mystery. Truth was, there was something fishy about the whole thing that I couldn't quite place my finger on. My mother was nonplussed, walking just far enough away that she could have a private phone call, but not too far away that I couldn't listen in if I wanted.

I didn't. Either she'd find Dostarious's twin—an ancient ex-vampire by the name of Lizile, according to Charlie—or she wouldn't. As she dialed whomever she felt comfortable enough to wake this early in the morning, I checked my own phone. Reconnected to the network, it buzzed three times back to back, indicating that I had two missed calls from Justin and one from Egya. No messages, and judging from the evenly spaced-out times they called, I guessed they were just checking in on us.

I thought about calling back, but it was so late—well, early, by now —they had to be asleep. Or trying to sleep. Either way, I figured it best to give them a few hours before calling.

So I put my phone and half an amulet in my pants pockets (1970s chinos, gotta love the pocket space!) and watched as my mother talked on the phone, pacing back and forth in that nervous little waddle of hers. Her movements reminded me of when I was a child and she'd walk up and down our little cabin when she was nervous about something.

And watching that same shuffle brought back a flood of memories I thought I had buried long ago.

↔↔↔

Old Scotland—The Day Katrina Darling Died

Turning isn't like it is in the movies. I wish it were, but when you're bitten, or rather *infected*, it's just like fighting off any particularly bad flu. You have good days and bad days, but overall you're heading in a downward spiral.

Except a downward spiral in this case doesn't look like you're getting worse. To the untrained eye, you look like you're getting better—healthier. You can move, you're in less pain, your fever subsides and your strength slowly returns.

Those are the other symptoms—the ones that mean you're getting worse.

The more telling symptoms—the ones you should be on the lookout for, if you somehow knew what you were looking for—are an aberrance to light, weight loss and not eating—as in *ever*.

I didn't know what was happening to me, but my vampiric instincts were kicking in, and they were telling me to hide the more telling symptoms as best I could. So I pretended to eat. I asked that my bed be positioned so that direct sunlight never touched it (using a desire to be able to look through my bedroom door and into the house as an excuse). I also pretended to be weaker than I was.

Like I said, I didn't know what was happening to me. All I did know was that whatever it was, it was going to change me forever. For eternity. At least until the gods up and left, but that wouldn't come for another three hundred years.

What are the symptoms for those who do *not* get worse? Simple: the fever takes hold, you fall deeper and deeper into a coma and eventually you die.

Once you are bitten, you will eventually die. Whether you come back as a vampire or not.

And that is perhaps the greatest gift the gods gave us by leaving. The bite no longer kills.

↔

As the day progressed, so too did my strength grow, and much more quickly than I let on. My father didn't notice; he was too distracted with relief that his little girl wasn't going to die after all. My mother, however, noticed the little feats of strength that I didn't hide as well as I should have.

Little things like pushing my heavy oak bed out of the path of direct sunlight or bringing in a bucket to better hide the food I wasn't eating. I was sloppy, sure, but I could feel my body literally dying. Can you blame me?

She finally realized that I wasn't eating. At all. In those early days, solid food was repulsive. I could tolerate raw meat, but barely. And as for vegetables, the thought of swallowing a potato or carrot was as physically repulsive to me then as the thought of sucking blood from the carotid artery of a human is to me now.

Life's strange like that. Death, too.

Given that this was eighteenth century Scotland, meat wasn't something you ate every day, farmer or no. Meat was far too valuable on the open market, so our diet was mostly comprised of potatoes, carrots, leeks and oats. In other words, food that vampires are practically allergic to. And not an EpiPen in sight. (Tasteless joke, that. Maybe I'll dissect my morbid sense of humor in my Psych class …)

Anyway, I got very good at hiding my food. Or so I thought. For the most part, what I did was place it in my bedpan (thankfully, because I wasn't putting anything *in* my body, nothing was coming *out*, either) and bury it in the garden when my parents slept.

This went on for a few days until my mother—the shrewd bitch that she is—asked me to join my father and her at the dinner table.

I tried to feign an excuse that I was still too weak and tired. My father even intervened in his way, asking Mother to be gentle on the poor girl who nearly died not three weeks before.

"Pish, posh," my mother said, waving away our objections like one might chase away an enterprising bee disturbing your picnic. "She's fine. Come, darling, sit with us."

We both saw the resolve in my mother's eyes and knew resistance was futile (hah—my mother was the original Borg). I continued to feign weakness and my doting father came to my side, helping me to a seat at the dinner table.

"Eat, darling," my mother said, putting a large ladle-sized helping of boiled porridge on my plate. I could have gagged.

"No, thank you—I'm not hungry."

"Nonsense. You've eaten every dinner we've given you so far. Why is now any different?"

"All the movement," I said. "I fear the walk from my bedroom to here has tired me. Father—will you help me back to bed?"

My father placed his hands on the table to help himself stand, as was his wont now, so that he could assist me. But before he could right himself, my mother whacked his hand with her ladle. "Sit."

"Charlotte—what is the meaning of this?" my father said, rubbing the back of his hand.

"Our daughter claims that she was weakened by the walk from that room"—she pointed at my bedroom door—"to here. And yet, she is not too weak to bury *these* every night."

Walking over to a basket near the main room's hearth, she opened its lid, exposing all the food I had buried over the last few days. It was spoiled now, filled with maggots and worms, midges and other insects best left in the dirt.

"She has not eaten anything in ten days and yet she looks as healthy as any young lady her age."

My father looked at the basket of food, speechless. Then he turned his gaze on me, a dawning realization darkening his face.

"But that is not all," my mother said, walking to the window behind me. I was frozen in place, horrified but unable to will myself to stop her. She pulled open the shades and sunlight hit my back with the same physical impact a cart or bull might muster.

At that point in my transformation I had yet to be exposed to direct sunlight, my vampiric instincts having told me to avoid the light at all costs. And so when the warm rays of the early afternoon sun scalded my porcelain skin, I leapt and did something that—at the time—I did not know was possible. Cat-like claws extended from my fingers and I hung onto the ceiling of our cabin as if I were crawling on the ground.

That was not the only change the ambush of sunlight brought upon me. Now that the monster inside was exposed, it also showed its fangs. I hungered for the one substance on this good, green Earth that would sustain me.

Blood.

And below me stood two humans with enough blood for me to feast on for days.

Every muscle, fiber, thought and desire I possessed told me to leap at them. More than that—it gave me a strategy. Go for my father first —hobble him by severing his Achilles heel. Once he was down, do the same to my mother. With the two of them hobbled, take your time. Savor the drink.

You deserve it.

Truly you do.

Those were what my instincts told me; my heart, fortunately, was a very different story. What I saw below me were the two people I loved more than anything else in this world or any other. And when my eyes locked with my father's, and I saw the pain in him, the pain caused by saving and then damning his only daughter for eternity, I knew that I could no more hurt them now than I could run into the light and end it all.

I dropped from the ceiling into a dark corner of the room and began to cry.

Nay—to say the expression of pain that came out of me was simply *crying* is to say that the ocean is filled with a single teaspoon of water. I didn't simply cry. I howled. I grieved. I wailed.

I lamented.

The mind is a funny thing. In those tears I momentarily forgot why I was crying, and my thoughts were thus filled with a deeper hurt.

Why, thought I, weren't my parents coming forth to comfort me?

That was their way. Their lot. To scoop me up when I fell, to hold me when I grieved. To love me unconditionally.

Looking up at them I saw love in my father's eyes. I also saw confusion and hate and rage and fear. I think it was that last expression that hurt me the most. Vampire or not, I would never hurt him. Couldn't he see that?

At least that was what I believed in that moment.

In my mother's eyes I did not see the same raw mix of emotions. Her eyes were, instead, hollow. Empty.

After a long moment, I finally managed to get my own emotions under control. "It's not my fault," I said.

They were the only words I could think to say.

So I chose to be silent, and we all sat in it. Blessed silence.

But the blessed are only blessed for so long before the good fortune leaves to aid another. Our blessed silence was broken by three simple words spoken by my mother.

"Cast—her—*out.*"

↔

Despite my mother's commands to do so, my father did not cast me out. Not immediately. He knew that the light would burn me, and having mercy on me—or perhaps unable to reconcile his guilt for not arriving sooner and saving me from such a fate—he let me stay in the dark corner of our little, once-happy home until dark.

In that time, I sat silent. My mother paced, careful not to get too close to me. My father ... my father just sat there, his eyes burning through me as if he were trying to work out the formula to an impossible equation.

I did not move from my corner for hours, even after the sun set. I suppose I had hoped that if I was quiet enough, good enough, they would let me stay.

But Hope is a fickle bitch, only gracing the very few she deems worthy. An hour after sunset, my father hobbled to my corner and offered me his hand.

"Harold," my mother cried out, "she is not to be trusted. She's a monster, an animal, a—"

"*Enough,* Charlotte!" he yelled, whipping around to face her. Then, shaking his head, loosing a tear from between closed eyelids, he whispered, "Enough."

He held out his hand again and eventually, seeing no other choice, I took it. Gently helping me to my feet, he guided me out of the front door of a home that I once called my own. Never again, I knew.

Outside, he gave me one last look as a final tear rolled down his cheek and quietly, lovingly closed the door. With that gesture, my father made it perfectly clear.

I was no longer his daughter.

I was no longer welcome in his home.

I was a monster.

Cast out and alone, I did what any no-good creature of the night does ... I sulked off into the darkness where monsters like me belonged.

And I cried some more.

10

TRUTH YOU CAN'T EAT

"*Excellent!*" My mother's cheerful voice brought me back to the present day with a crash. She was frantically writing something down while simultaneously trying to keep the phone to her ear, hold her purse and walk toward me.

She managed her awkward multitasking quadrathlon quite well. Evidently she got what she wanted, hanging up the phone, letting it drop in her purse before handing me a piece of paper with an address on it. "I found Lizile's address, and wonderful, *wonderful* news! *Excellent* news! She lives not six hours from here. Thank the GoneGods for small miracles, even when such things no longer exist. Six hours. We could be there by lunch!"

My mother gave me a smile like she just won the lottery.

I didn't return it. My memories of those three words still echoed in my head.

Cast ... her ... out.

"We?" I asked.

That one little word wiped away the smile from my mother's face. Attempting to save face, she rolled her eyes. "We, me, you—whatever and whoever—*someone* can be there by lunch."

"So go," I said.

I half expected some protest. Some snide retort. But instead she simply held out her hand.

I stared at it. "What?"

"The amulet—half of it, at least. I need it."

"What? Not coming back once you retrieve the other half?"

My mother shook her head. "Best I keep going and get the whole thing to HQ. Besides, we never know when those Cherub nuts might strike again."

"Indeed," I said, scanning her face for some betrayal of what she was really thinking. I saw nothing and had to admit that she could possibly mean what she was saying. And yet …

Cast … her … out.

My mother continued to hold out her hand. I continued to stare.

Until eventually: "OK, Mother—I'll give you the amulet … but you have to do something for me first."

Another eyeroll. "What?"

I smiled. I'd finally found my ace. "There's someone I'd like you to meet. An Other named Mergen. He's kind of a legend around here."

↔

Mergen was the avatar of the Turkish god of wisdom. In other words —whenever someone on Earth was lucky (or unlucky, depending on what you did) to meet one of the Turkish gods, you never got to meet the actual guy. You met their avatar.

Next best thing? Possibly. But just because you're only meeting a god's avatar, doesn't make the experience any less powerful. Or weird.

And when it came to Mergen, weird was what you got. You see, Mergen didn't eat food, drink blood or soak up sunrays for nourishment. He ate Truth—the real stuff, with a capital T.

Tell him a lie—anything, really, that wasn't the Truth, the Whole

Truth, So Help You, God—and he'd groan like he just took a sip of sour milk. Tell him the truth—the *Truth*—and he'd smack his lips in exquisite joy. The bigger the truth, the happier he is. Same goes for the other way.

In other words, he's a human lie-detector.

I took my mother to the alleyway behind McGill's bookstore, the avatar's usual haunt. Sure enough, there was the nearly translucent, white Other sitting on a cardboard slat. He wore traditional Turkish garb that made him look like the father in *Aladdin* and was reading a stack of Harlequin Romances. Egya asked him about that once. Supposedly those little trashy books contained more truth about love, sex and relationships than you'd think. And judging by how plump he was these days, he was getting a lot of Truth out of this batch.

"Mother, meet Mergen."

She looked at him, then me, before extending a careful hand. "Hello, Mr. Mergen. Pleasure to meet you."

Mergen, instead of taking the proffered hand, groaned in dissatisfaction.

"Interesting response," my mother whispered to me, retracting her hand.

"He's eccentric, Mother, but he is *brilliant*. No one knows more about magical artifacts than he does."

At this, he groaned again, making a "yuk" face. He knew about as much about magical items as I did. I ignored this—my mother wouldn't know what he meant by that—pulled out the amulet half from my purse and handed it to him. "What can you make of this, Mergen?"

Mergen looked at it, confused.

"My mother says it can ..." I turned to her. "How did you phrase it?"

Instead, she glanced at him dubiously. "Are you sure we can trust him?"

"With my life," I said.

At this he smiled, smacking his lips. Which seemed to only unsettle Mother more, much to my delight.

"Very well," she sighed. "Once activated it will help us know where the gods went and why."

Mergen made a sour face, which my mother hopefully interpreted to mean that he, too, thought the knowledge too great for any one person to have.

"Don't worry," I said to him, playing along. "My mother knows people."

"Indeed—my organization will protect it."

At this, surprisingly, Mergen smiled.

OK—so far one in the lie column, one in the truth column. *Let's dig.*

"Mother, do you have any idea how it works?"

My mother shook her head. "From what I understand, you have to ask it the right questions. It will only answer with the knowledge it possesses, but I'm told this is almost infinite."

Mergen rubbed his tummy in satisfaction. Mother took a small step backward, as if sickened by him.

"I also know," she went on, "that there is a difference between what you *want* to be true and what is actually True. It will tell you both—and you have to decide which one you will follow. That is why it is so dangerous."

Judging from Mergen's pleased look, more Truth.

So far my mother was hitting it out of the park. Everything she said was true except one thing—what the amulet actually revealed. I also had proof that she knew it wouldn't do what she told us it would … I knew this because Mergen can only tell when you are lying. If my mother actually *believed* the amulet possessed the knowledge of where the gods went and why, Mergen would not have reacted the way he did at her answer.

"Mergen," I said, "any idea how it works?"

The avatar just shrugged.

"OK." I about-faced, facing my mother, and folded my arms. "Mother, one last question … what does the amulet actually do? No more games. And no more lies."

↔

"Darling, whatever do you mean?"

"I mean that you are lying to me … well, actually you're telling me a lot of true stuff … but you're lying about the knowledge the amulet possesses. It doesn't know where the gods are, does it?"

"Darling—again, *what* are you talking about …?" Her voice trailed off as she looked down at Mergen. "You, ghost man … who are you?"

"Mergen. I already told you."

"Not you, darling, *him*. Answer me."

Mergen just looked up, sucking air between his teeth. It took me a long time to know how to talk to this guy. It would take my mother even long—

"My name is Charlotte Darling," she said.

Mergen narrowed his eyes.

"Fine, my name *was* Charlotte McMahon, but some years after turning into a vampire, I changed it to Charlotte Darling so that my daughter and I could still have … a connection. After all, vampire or not, we were still flesh and blood."

He smacked his lips.

"I'm a famous ballerina."

At this Mergen crunched up his face in distaste.

"I see …" she said. "You are a clever little girl, aren't you? Using this poor creature in our little games. You are so sure I'm lying to you that you will stoop to all manners of deception yourself to just catch me in a single half-truth."

At this Mergen began chewing—loudly—before belching—also loudly.

"Very well, my precious little darling, you want the truth, you shall have it. This amulet is a map, and when I said it will tell us about where the gods went, that was half the truth. It will, more accurately, indicate where the magic they left behind *is*—"

Mergen began to make dissatisfied noises, but before he could grace us with a full reaction, my mother held a finger up to his face and snapped, "And before you give us your reaction, let me finish. It will indicate where some of the magic is. In other words, it will allow its user access to a well of magic that can be used for evil."

At this Mergen's face relaxed and eventually brightened.

"This map, in the wrong hands, can disrupt the balance of power."

Mergen gave us an appreciative sigh.

"And, before I get accused of lying again, let me say that it might be a significant clue into where the gods went and why."

I looked down at Mergen and noted that not only did he look like he was having the best meal of his life, but he was also holding his hand out, gesturing like he couldn't eat another bite.

Seeing his reaction was like a slap in the face because it meant that I was wrong.

My mother was telling the truth.

Miracles really did still happen.

↔

There are few tortures I can't take. I should know—I've been drowned, skewered like a kabob with red-hot metal, punched, kicked ... I've even had my nails pulled out by a particularly nasty pixie in Dublin one drunken night about forty years ago.

I would happily trade any of those with the look of "I told you so" my mother was currently throwing at me.

"Satisfied?"

I didn't answer.

"Satisfied?" Her voice was louder now.

I nodded. Reluctantly.

"Good. Do you have anything to say to your mama?"

"I'm sorry," I whispered, looking at the ground.

"Come again? I didn't hear you."

"I'm sorry," I said, louder.

My mother looked over at Mergen, who was busy picking his teeth. "Yes," she said, "I can see that you are. Very well—would you like to know how you can make it up to me?"

I nodded, not sure if I really did. Thankfully she didn't look at Mergen for confirmation.

"Come with me. We'll make it our little mother-daughter bonding road trip."

"Fine," I said. "Let me just call the boys and check up on them."

I pulled out my phone and, groaning at how early it still was, dialed Justin's number. No answer. I dialed Egya's, and it rang four times before someone picked up.

And it wasn't Egya.

11

SOMETIMES ALL IT TAKES IS A PHONE CALL

"Who is this?" I asked, putting the phone on speaker.

"Who do you think this is?" the voice hissed back. "We have your friends, which puts me in a strange situation. You see, at first I thought I'd interrogate them to find out where you are. But then I saw how much the two of them did nae want to tell me anything and figured that you tricked them into loving you."

Did nae? Who still talks like that? Shaking aside the thought, I growled into the phone, "If you hurt them—"

"Good—that's all the confirmation I need to know that you care about them. We're at the Rust Yard. From what I know, it's a pretty famous place. Come and get them. You have three hours and then you need not be in a rush anymore, if you catch me meaning."

Click.

He was gone.

↔

"Let's go, darling," my mother said, gently grabbing my arm. Her "I told you so" tone had vanished.

"This makes no sense. Divine Cherubs don't hurt civilians. Why would they take Justin and Egya?"

"A lot can change in a few hundred years. Rogue factions can emerge. Man's heart is corruptible … is it really that hard to imagine that the Cherubs would become more violent, more"—she searched for the word—"evil?"

"But …" I narrowed my eyes. "And that accent—did it strike you as familiar?"

She shrugged. "We've both spent many lifetimes traveling. All accents are familiar in some sense."

"He also said … 'did nae.' You heard that, right? Who talks like that?"

Another shrug. "Scots, Irish—romantics."

I shook my head slowly, thinking. "No, it's more than that. I sensed a bit of Scottish twang there."

"Like I said—Scots, Irish, romantics."

I shook my head more vehemently. "You don't understand. I didn't just hear a Scottish accent. I heard an *Inverness* one. Just like the one from home … but not Inverness *now*. Inverness from when we were human."

"We *are* human, darling."

"No, Mother. From when we were human *three hundred years ago.*"

At this my mother scoffed. "Darling. A Scottish accent I can give you. I'll even go along with Inverness, although I doubt that. But Inverness from when we were first human? That's ridiculous. Patently absurd! You don't even have an accent from Inverness anymore. Neither do I."

My mother was right. Over the centuries I'd lost my accent, turning it into a hodgepodge of dialects from around the world. I doubted I could turn on my childhood accent even if I wanted to.

"Darling—come, let's go."

I nodded. "OK, but the Rust Yard is an hour by bus. We'll need a car—"

"No, darling, not the Rust Yard. To Lizile. She's only six hours away."

"What? We have to save—"

"You said it yourself. Cherubs don't hurt civilians. They'll let the boys go once they know we're not coming."

"Divine Cherubs don't *kidnap* civilians, either. Egya and Justin are in real danger—"

"And you will only get them into more trouble by trying to help."

I turned my hard eyes on her. "You mean like you did by showing up?"

She sighed and stopped trying to pull me along. "Darling, I didn't know I was being stalked by those unbalanced hunters. If I had, I would have been more cautious."

"But you said that you were in danger. That people were following you."

"And they are, but they are months behind me. I made sure of it."

I rolled my eyes. "That's reassuring."

She gave me another, more patient sigh. "Look, I've changed. In the game of cloak and dagger, I am more cloak these days. You live longer."

"OK—so the danger you thought was trailing you isn't here. But danger still followed you and you're responsible for helping settle the consequences."

"I might be, darling, but I'm also responsible for getting the amulet and helping many more people than just Justin and Egya—as handsome as the former and charming as the latter may be."

It was in that moment that literally hundreds of years of frustration came pouring out of me.

"I thought you *changed*, Mother, but clearly you haven't. Always looking out for yourself, throwing others in prison in your place and throwing away the key once you've had your way with them."

She blinked. She looked genuinely confused—which wasn't the emotional response I was looking to elicit.

"No, darling, I am *thinking*. Something you should try, I might add. And before you can come back at me with some platitude," she said, lifting a silencing hand, "here are my thoughts. Divine Cherubs do not hurt civilians. We have no reason to think that this particular group is anything more than slightly more enterprising, gung-ho Cherubs who will do the right thing and let them go.

"But even if they are not, my mission will save thousands of lives. Possibly more. To put my mission and the amulet—half it may be—in danger would be irresponsible."

Great, my mother is lecturing me on being responsible.

"I am, indeed," she said, either reading my thoughts or benefiting from my mind-mouth filter.

"I don't need your lecture—nor do I need your help," I said, fishing for the amulet in my pocket. I threw it at her and stalked away. "You go be 'responsible,' if that's what you call it. I'll go do what's *right*."

And with that, I left.

If only I wasn't so furious, so out of control with rage, I would have paused to look at Mergen in that moment and see what he thought of our little conversation. But I didn't.

Had I done so, I would have never given my mother that damn amulet.

12

CHANGELINGS, BABY RATS, BROADSWORDS AND BAD-ASSARY

I returned to my dorm room barely conscious of how I got there. All I could see was a thick fog of red hate.

Deirdre was there, still nursing her rat-cubs, still buck-ass naked. I paused long enough to wonder if she had tried to nurse them the more natural way, instead of relying on toy baby bottles. Best not to think of it.

Quickly, I rummaged through the hidden compartment in the false ceiling. I was looking for my dirk and my father's Cherub mask.

They weren't the only ones who could fight like angels.

Putting on my kilt and leather jacket, I was ready to do some serious harm.

I turned to see that Deirdre was no longer naked. Instead she was wearing dark green tights and a black T-shirt so tight it left little to the imagination. She had spread mud that she got from only the GoneGods knew where over her face and arms. If that was it, I would have thought she was going out for a walk. No telling what passes as fashion for changelings.

But the tell-tale, neon-friggin'-sign that she was dressed for much more than a leisurely stroll through nature was the giant broadsword held aloft with one muscle-corded arm.

"Who needs slaying and where?" she asked.

University. They say you'll make your best friends here.

They were right.

↔

The Rust Yard was a graveyard for ships just outside of the city. Back in the day, ships would come up the St. Lawrence, dropping off cargo as they went. Montreal, being one of the last stops (or first stops, depending on your direction) also served as a repair dock for big metal cargo boats.

But back in the 1930s, it was often cheaper to replace than repair, and soon the massive lot near Old Montreal became a place where ships met a landlocked death.

After the big war—number 2, not 1—industries changed, railways were built, and fewer ships came here. Eventually ports were moved to the north of the city where a convenient highway had sprung up, and this shipyard became a desert of rusting boats—hence the nickname Rust Yard.

Over the years, people tried to do a lot with this place. Paintball, raves, a museum, an artisan fair … you name it, people tried it. But the Rust Yard was just too far out of the city and didn't have any four-lane highways going its way, so eventually everything they tried went the way of the ships and died.

Such is life. And death, I suppose. GoneGods, that's morbid.

Deirdre and I made it to the Rust Yard about forty minutes before the three-hour deadline. Good—that would give us plenty of time to scope out the place and decide the best course of action.

Figuring that they'd have all the gates into the place monitored, we opted to climb the fence. Problem was that a few years back, after some college kid was killed when a boat fell on him, the city erected thirty-foot-high metal mesh fences with barbwire at the top. Granted, the college kid had been tripping on LSD at the time, and had been attacking the boat's stand repeatedly for hours with a metal baseball bat, but that didn't seem to matter; they turned a relatively easy place to get inside into a relatively difficult place to break-and-enter.

Luckily I had the foresight to bring wire cutters with me. Or, in this case, a broadsword-wielding changeling.

"Deirdre, my changeling warrior, do you mind?"

"Not at all," she said, and heaved up her sword with a mighty—

"Deirdre—quietly. We're being sneaky, remember?"

She looked down at her Nikes and said in a very matter-of-fact tone, "I know. That is why I wore my sneakers."

I had to restrain myself from slapping my forehead. The changeling was constantly making little mistakes about human culture. Little errors based on assumptions she made or taking things too literally. And for some reason I felt responsible for correcting her.

"Deirdre, honey—they're not called sneakers because they're designed for *sneaking*."

Deirdre looked disappointed. "Was I not funny?"

"Oh!" I said, now pleasantly surprised. "That was a *joke*. You said it in such a flat tone that I missed it."

"Not flat, dry. You are from the British Empire and the British sense of humor is dry. Like a martini."

She smiled at this joke, and before I could respond she thrust her broadsword through one of the mesh fence's holes and pushed. The threading split apart. I noted that Deirdre wasn't pushing very hard. Either she was incredibly strong, or that broadsword was razor sharp. I suspected it was a combination of the two.

Once the hole was sufficiently widened, she crawled the sword up and around, making a Katrina-sized hole for me to walk through.

How considerate.

↔

Inside, we bolted to a nearby ship for cover. The ghostly ships that littered the graveyard were placed quite close to one another (I guess the 1930s killed a lot of boats) and so cover wasn't an issue as we made our way through in broad daylight.

But just because we got lucky with cover didn't mean we were *lucky*. There was easily five hundred ships, trawlers, cargo boats, skiffs and other vessels of varying sizes here, and our kidnappers could be in any one. There were also a half dozen buildings, abandoned offices and warehouses, all ideal for holding two humans captive.

Finding them will take luck, if not—

"Not luck, milady. Sacrifice." She pulled off her backpack and picked up her three pups. They were so small and hairless that they couldn't have been more than three days old.

Deirdre cradled them in her arms and began whispering, "When I found you and took you in my loving embrace, I took the place of your dead mother. You are my responsibility now. That was a mistake, my loved ones, because I cannot keep you long enough for you to grow strong and wise. I cannot keep you long enough for you to learn what you must to survive. But just because I cannot keep you, does not mean I will abandon you."

I watched as the changeling, with her unblemished skin (minus the mud) and impossible youth began to grow older. Tiny but unmistakable marks of age appeared on her face. A skin tag, a mole, three liver spots.

She was burning time.

"Stop!"

But before I could even reach out to her, she opened up her arms, revealing the pups—who were no longer pups at all, but young rats, not quite fully grown, but big enough to scare the beejeezus out of me.

"Mama!" I yelped.

The changeling looked at her pups and giggled.

"Deirdre, what did you do? How much time did you burn?"

"A year."

"A year! For rats?"

"A year for three children who were my responsibility. Seems fair. More than fair."

I looked at the changeling who smiled down at her—what? children?—and could see genuine tears of relief and pride.

When the gods left, every creature OnceImmortal was now made mortal. Different creatures had different life spans that mostly depended on how powerful they were. It was said that angels had a thousand years, archangels closer to ten thousand. Pixies could live up to two hundred years, and gargoyles less than eighty. These once divine creatures, although mortal, were not stripped of their magical abilities. They were, however, hobbled. Life and magic are intrinsically tied together, and so if an Other wishes to use his or her magic, they must give up some of their life to do it.

One other thing that the gods did to Others beside make them mortal: Others cannot have children. So no replenishing of the species, no living on through DNA. Once a species of Other died, they died forever.

This already happened. The Scottish brownies were only given two years and, since the gods left four years ago, they had all died out. The first of the divine creatures to go extinct in this GoneGod world. And surely not the last.

Life was precious, and even though Deirdre probably had a lot of years in her, I doubted she would see half of them. Deirdre was too good not to use her magic to help others and Others alike.

Deirdre snuggled the rats, showering each one of them with kisses, before saying, "Go, be free. Live. Survive. Thrive. But before you leave me, can Mommy ask you for one small favor?"

↔

The newly-made-adolescent rats scurried through the Rust Yard like bats out of hell. Well, *rats* out of hell. With their sense of smell and speed, they found where Egya and Justin were being held within minutes.

The Divine Cherubs were holding the boys in the warehouse closest to the water. Made sense. Farthest from the main entrance, closest to the water—which, if they were smart, offered them an escape route. I was guessing that they probably had some little speed boat ready and waiting just in case, and as we approached the building from the shoreline, I saw I was right.

A speed boat ready and facing outward.

And from our vantage point, I could see two of the Cherubs—masks still on—standing near two very frightened humans duct taped to chairs.

Well, one frightened human. Egya was smiling, as usual.

↔

Egya's wicked smile gave me an equally wicked plan, which I quickly shared with Deirdre as we sat by the shore.

The changeling nodded. "You would have made a formidable general in the fae army."

High compliment coming from a fae warrior indeed, and I curtsied in thanks.

Without another word, Deirdre sheathed her broadsword and began running along the shoreline to her destination.

I paused for a moment, taking in my surroundings. This was something I did before every battle. A moment to center myself before kicking some butt. The moon hung full in the sky, illuminating the beauty of the river. A pretty idyllic place to be, if it weren't for my boyfriend bound to a chair (instead of a bed) and three homicidal Divine Cherubs wanting to kill me.

"OK ... time to fight fire with fire," I muttered to myself.

And I put on my father's Cherub mask.

13

WANNA DANCE, MY LITTLE ANGEL?

J was running up along the side of the hangar. (Do you call boat warehouses "hangars"? I'd look it up on my phone if I weren't—you know—in the middle of a mission.) Once I was where I needed to be, I started counting to one hundred to make sure Deirdre was in position.

1 …

2 …

3 …

Trouble with counting is your mind tends to wander.

53 …

After I rescue them, how am I going to explain all this to Justin?

59 …

I'll have to tell him everything and hope he doesn't tell me to jump into a lake. Or go to hell. Or worse—stop kissing me.

62 …

Justin's going to hate me, isn't he?

68 …

Egya knows and understands and doesn't care.

77 …

Why can't Justin be more like Egya?

81 ...

Because he was never bitten, duh. He's just an ordinary boy.

84 ...

An ordinary boy who deserves an ordinary girl.

89 ...

Screw that!

90 ...

Ordinary's boring.

91 ...

I'm anything but—once I tell him everything, he'll understand.

92 ...

Won't he?

95 ...

No, he won't!

99 ...

Why not? It's not like I asked to be a vampire.

102 ...

I was bitten. No fault of my own.

106 ...

Besides, if I wasn't bitten I would have died and never met him.

109 ...

So in a way he should be grateful I'm a vampire!

110 ...

And aren't I risking my life to save him?

111—

Oh shoot, I missed my count. Time to make up for lost time ...

I charged at the A-frame holding up the front of a large fishing boat that looked like it could have been a prop in *Forrest Gump*. I put all my lighter-than-a-stack-of-newspapers weight behind the shove, hoping to dislodge the damn thing. Given how big it was, I figured I might have to do a couple runs to get it to move.

I was wrong. The thing crumbled under my first hit and I barely had enough time to tumble out from under the boat and to the other side. It came crashing down like a—well, like a boat crashing off of its stand in a dirt lot.

A loud *BANG!* accompanied the fall. Before the noise could settle, I shimmied up its side and got into position. It didn't take long for the Cherubs to come outside, and once they were out in the open, I stood up and pointed my dirk at them.

"You two have defied the code of the Divine Cherubs. Kidnapping civilians and using them as bait is not our way," I said.

I figured the sight of me in my father's mask would give me enough distraction to cause them pause. I was right—and not surprising, if I'm being honest; I had a lot of practice throwing gravitas into my words back in my vampiring days.

These two froze for a solid ten seconds as they looked up at me standing there in my mask. Then one of them spoke.

"The mask. How did you get it?"

"What do you mean? I'm a Divine Cherub."

"What's a Divine Cherub?" asked the younger of the two.

"What's a Divine Cherub? You've got to be kidding me. What do you think that mask on your face represents? A baby-shower catering group?"

"But Simione said that we were Angel Fighters," one said.

The other turned to him and replied, "I wanted to be called Fallen Angels or Hell's Angels, but he said that both names were already taken."

I cut in. "Simione?" The name was familiar somehow, but before I could place it, I felt a hard kick to my back.

"You are no Cherub, child," said the largest man of the three, stepping up behind me. "You are a monster barely fit to be crushed beneath my boot."

I could see the same crisp green eyes burning with hatred as he pushed a very heavy boot down on my chest, and as he did so he muttered, "The god of peace will soon crush Satan under your shoe."

The pain was instant. I could feel him literally crushing the breath out of me, and still he pushed. I heard a rib crack. Hell, it could have been three. I tried to pivot, sway, move. But I couldn't. He was strong and his boot so large that it stretched from navel to nipple. The fringes of my eyesight started to go dark. I was passing out, and if that happened, I would be done. This guy was not messing around.

In the distance I heard the rumble of an engine and knew that Deirdre had done her part. I also knew now that there was no help coming. I had made Deirdre swear that she would get them to safety. Oaths, promises, swears—the fae took them extremely seriously. Once the words were uttered, they would be followed. She had gotten the boys to the boat and they were speeding off to safety as my breath, too, was leaving me.

So, all in all, not a total loss, I thought as more of my sight burst into blackness.

Then I heard a judgmental, menthol-wafting voice reply:

"You're always so dramatic, darling."

PART III
INTERMISSION

When Charlotte Darling was a young vampire—only seventy-three years undead, practically a new-unborn—she was a careless vampire. She pillaged, plundered, killed and maimed, as is the wont of youth. But all that was par for course when you were a vampire. None of *that* was what made her careless.

What made her careless was her arson tendencies—metaphorically speaking. Charlotte Darling was a burner of bridges—again, metaphorically—ruining every relationship she ever forged with any vampire or creature of the night. Indeed, her relationship pyromania even extended to her own daughter and sire, whom she tried to kill at least once a decade from the day she first opened her eyes as a vampire all the way to the day the gods left.

She was this way for two reasons: one—when you lived forever and possessed immense power, very few of your actions had any real consequences to worry about; and two—she was a creature only capable of holding a single purpose, desire or mission in mind, whatever it may be.

And that single purpose, desire or mission needed to be achieved no matter who was hurt or killed, no matter what the damage, no matter how it was achieved.

But after the gods left, consequences became very real. So real, Charlotte—newly human, lost and alone—had no one to turn to. All her monstrous affiliations would not return her calls. Those bridges were metaphorical ash.

She was alone, alone, alone.

In the first GoneGod year in which she was newly made mortal, she wandered the streets, trying to drown her sorrow in shopping, drink and gambling, in no particular order. Eventually, she could no longer afford any of the three (unlike her daughter who saved, invested and planned, Charlotte didn't have much in the way of financial security).

Still alone and now broke, she was truly lost. So lost that she did something that no self-respecting vampire would ever consider.

She went to church.

Of course, after the gods left most churches had been reduced to community centers and traveling Other freakshows (and sometimes daycares), but the one she found was run by a particularly devote Catholic who happily took Charlotte's confessions.

And did she have much to confess.

The priest—who was also, as it happened, trained as a counselor—listened, taking his holy duties very seriously; but he also used his training to note something quite interesting about this once-vampire.

She was the true definition of "single-minded." So much so, he noted, that she must have some form of obsessive compulsive disorder. Of course, if she had been born in modern times, as opposed to eighteenth century Scotland, she would have been diagnosed much earlier. Instead of a few centuries after she was born.

The priest considered her circumstance. Being on the spectrum of OCD *and* being a vampire made her a very dangerous creature, he feared. For the former would give her an intense need to do whatever took hold in her mind and the latter would give her the power to get it done.

The priest contacted several newly made programs to help Others, explaining his ... ahhh ... *client*'s unique circumstances. Most calls led nowhere, until one day he got on the phone with a very ancient-sounding man with an accent so eclectic he could not even begin to place it.

"So," said the man on the other end of the phone, "you say that this Charlotte ...?"

"Let us leave it with 'Charlotte.' Client confidentiality, you understand," the priest said.

"I didn't know God was still *taking* clients," the voice rasped back. When the priest did not laugh, the voice said, "I have been told that my humor is off-putting. My apologies. So, this Charlotte ... she is mentally ill?"

"I wouldn't put it in such harsh terms. I merely observe that she has some form of OCD. Her challenges in this regard coupled with being a vampire—rather, a *former* vampire, a, say, born-again human —probably make her a formidable danger. My interest, however, has less to do with her ... she is doing quite well under my care, you understand ... my interest is that if she has these ... ahhh ... challenges, perhaps other Others do as well. We must look to our new arrivals' mental health. If not OCD, then PTSD—it is easy to theorize that getting kicked out of heaven can be quite stressful on—"

"I admire your passion. But first, a few questions about this Charlotte ... are you saying that once booned with a mission, she would see it to the bitter end?"

" 'Booned'?"

"Tasked, imbued, given ... she will see it through, using mind, heart and body?"

"If she believes that something is important, and takes it upon herself to get it done, then yes—mind, heart and body."

"Are you sure about her heart?"

"Mister ...?"

"Doctor. Dr. Torquemada."

"Dr. Torquemada. I'm not sure what your question is."

"Her heart, I wish to know about her *heart*. Will it carry her mission no matter what?"

The priest was losing patience with this Dr. Torquemada, and he didn't quite trust this line of questioning. Still, this was the only person he had spoken to who actually took an interest in Charlotte and her needs. Perhaps this man with his raspy voice and undefinable accent could be a gateway to more responses so that he could help more Others.

With a heavy, inaudible sigh, the priest said, "If you mean that she will fully embrace her mission and have no doubt in its need to be completed ... then yes, her heart will carry it, too. But really, if we could discuss the larger problem—"

The line cut.

The priest briefly considered calling back but decided against it; this Dr. Torquemada was single-minded in his questions, so much so that the priest thought that perhaps he, too, was on the spectrum.

↔

It was Sunday, which meant that it was confession day. And given that in her weeks of confession, she had only managed to tell him about her first fifty years, she had a long way to go.

Dressing in an old Sunday dress—the one with thistles and roses— and collecting her parasol, she walked to the church, through its doors and into the confessional.

The divider that stood between priest and penitent slid open, but instead of the usual, kind and patient voice of the priest, she heard a raspy old thing say, "Hello, Charlotte."

"Where is the priest?"

"Priest?"

"Father ... erm ..." And Charlotte was horrified to discover that she had never learned the man's name. It was perhaps the first time in her life or death that she had come so close to questioning her own character. She finished weakly, "The man who is always here. My priest."

"Ahhh, yes, him," the voice rasped. "He is ... indisposed."

Charlotte knew enough to understand what "indisposed" meant. She had *indisposed* many herself. Wondering if this was some sort of vendetta—or worse, a crazed Other hunter—Charlotte sought to stand up and leave.

But as her hand reached for the purple curtain, the voice rasped, "Wait. Before you run, my *darling* ... let me ask you one question."

Charlotte hesitated. This man clearly wanted to speak to her, had been waiting for her. Anyone going through so much trouble would clearly have someone waiting outside the confessional to intercept should she decide to run.

Realizing she was trapped, Charlotte sat down in the chair.

"I'm listening," she said.

"The priest tells me that you are struggling with your current circumstances."

"If by circumstance, you mean *being human*, then yes." The words came out deadly serious, even though Charlotte meant it as a joke.

"I understand. What if I were to tell you that I have a remedy for the difficulties you face ... and all it requires is that you go on a little, shall we say, *mission*. Would you do it?"

14

BOOTS, PUPS AND BUTTERFLIES

"*Y*ou're always so dramatic, darling."

Those familiar words were followed by the loud thud of a two-by-four striking the back of the Divine Cherub's head.

He dropped, his foot no longer pressing down on my chest. Thank the GoneGods for small miracles.

My mother reached out a hand and helped me to my feet. The pain was agonizing. Standing, I realized that I had three broken ribs. At least. Jumping down from the boat, let alone escaping the Rust Yard, would be impossible.

As for fighting—shit. We were in trouble. Given how strong these Cherubs were—or Angel Fighters or whatever they called themselves —I doubted I could take them at full health, let alone injured. At least one of them was down already, I confirmed, looking over at the limp body on the dirt.

"Thank you, Mother," I said begrudgingly.

"Think nothing of it, darling. I'm just a mother trying to do the right thing."

I looked over the edge of the boat we were perched on and saw that the other two Cherubs were on the move. They might have been temporarily confused by my mask, but once they saw their leader attack me, well, they understood which angel to follow.

They were climbing up the edge of the boat and would be onboard in seconds. We were screwed.

If only we had more time, I thought, *just a few more seconds to figure something out.*

And as if the GoneGods were listening, my prayers were answered in the form of the three Reynolds rats: Captain Excellent, Hannibal King and Van Wilder. And they weren't adolescents anymore. They were tomcat-sized mega-rats, with armadillo-like armor for skin and raptor-style claws. (I wish I was joking, but I'm not.)

Seems that Deirdre, still taking my oath very seriously, found a loophole. She might not be able to help me, but her rat-pups could. And given how protective she was of her little darlings, she had burned some more time to get them battle ready.

I simultaneously felt guilt and admiration for my socially awkward changeling friend and vowed never to get frustrated with her constant questions and confusion. (Sadly, that was a vow I never kept.)

Van Wilder knocked the smaller of the two off the boat as Hannibal King took down the larger Cherub. Captain Excellent, meanwhile, stood vigil over their unconscious leader, roaring a challenge out to the world. I felt like I'd fallen right into some weird '80s crossover flick of *The Thing* and *Gremlins*.

We might have gotten out of the frying pan, but we weren't out of the fire—and the frying pan was full of corn oil that was popping meteor-sized boiling hot grease at us.

We had to get out of here and fast. Armadillo armor or not, the Cherubs would find a way to kill the rats, and Deirdre would never forgive me if that happened. The best thing to do was get away with the hope that Van Wilder, Hannibal King and Captain Excellent would be relieved from their duty and take the first opportunity of escape themselves.

"Come on, Mother, we've got to move."

"Darling," she said, looking at Captain Excellent. "What's *that?*"

"Captain Excellent," I said lamely. "Let's go!"

We moved to the front of the ship and hopped off. Well, my mother hopped off. I kind of fell with an agony that shot through me with every jolt of my body. We made it to the front of the yard where a Prius Hybrid stood, door open.

"Rental," my mother confirmed.

As I got into the passenger side, I could hear the screams of the Cherubs subsiding, which either meant the rats had stopped their attack, or they'd gotten the best of Deirdre's Ryan Reynolds trio. I hoped it was the former.

"Let's go," I said again.

My mother slammed on the accelerator and the car lurched forward at perfectly reasonable speed.

"You couldn't have gotten something with a little bit more kick?" I asked.

"No, darling, of course not. This car is the best they had, environment-wise. You can't compromise your principles just because someone is trying to kill you. Besides, the mileage is amazing."

15

PHONE CALLS, BROKEN CHESTS
AND A NEW RESPECT

*M*y mother pulled the Prius onto the highway and started making her way south—away from the Rust Yard, yes, but also away from downtown and, ultimately, McGill campus. From what I could tell, she was heading to the bridge that led off the island.

"Where are we going?" I asked. My ribs burned as I spoke; each little breath of air taken or expelled that forced my rib cage to expand or contract—however slightly—was seven layers of GoneGod hell.

How could a normal person bear this? Lucky for me, I had spent years (centuries) practicing the many forms of yoga, meditation, breathing techniques or even a little astral projection (although I never really got the knack of the whole out-of-body experience). Some of it I learned from the original masters, and the one thing they all talked about was managing pain, be it emotional or physical, through breath.

Closing my eyes, I started focusing on my breath as I waited for my mother to respond.

Nothing.

I opened my left eye and peeked at my mother. She was holding onto the steering wheel, obviously lost in thought as she maintained her cautious speed on the highway.

"Mother," I repeated, pleased that my centuries of practice had paid off. Now the pain was slightly oppressive, as opposed to excruciatingly unbearable.

"Yes, darling?" she said in the absent tone she used when she wasn't really listening to you and didn't care if you knew it or not.

"Where are we going?"

"To Lizile, darling. Where else?"

"Home? Well, *my* home. Or maybe, I don't know, hospital? I don't know if you've noticed, but I'm pretty banged up."

She peered over at me, and whatever she was thinking about went to the back of her mind as soon as she saw just how *banged up* I was.

"Darling," she said, worry painting every syllable of my nickname, "we have to fix you up!"

"Home, Mother. Home."

She shook her head. "Home is the last place you should be. They will go looking for you there. That will draw in more attacks. Not exactly the best medicine, if you ask me, though I'm no medical professional. Best we move on."

" 'Move on,' " I said, sitting up way too fast for my fractured ribs. "What do you mean, 'move on'?"

"Relax, darling. I don't mean forever. Just for a few days while we draw the heat off of us. Maybe my ... ahhh ... *people* can help us with our little Cherub problem. Once that is done, you can go back and study ... what are you studying, darling? I never asked."

"Others. Well, Other Public Policy, to be specific ... and, just for the record, I don't hate your plan," I said, shocked at my own words. *Must be the pain.*

"Pain or not, darling, I appreciate the sentiment." She gave my leg a light squeeze.

"OK—lay low for a few days. I suppose a spa is on the cards?"

My mother chuckled at this. "A spa—why not? But after, darling. First we got to—"

"Get the amulet. I know. Mother, you're like a dog with a bone."

"Thank you, darling," she said.

"For what?"

"Not saying what you're really thinking."

I raised a confused eyebrow.

"A *bitch* with a bone." She smiled. "That is what I would have said, at least."

↔

We drove for twenty minutes, my mother checking her rearview mirror every ten seconds or so, making sure we weren't being followed. From the constant sighs of relief, I gathered we weren't. But then again, I wasn't completely sure … I was too busy breathing.

I would have liked to continue my breathing exercises, but the real world has a way of getting in the way of a person doing something so simple. And the real world came crashing in on me in the form of a phone call.

My cell rang and my instinctual reaction was to reach for my bag. My spine did what it always does when bending down. My ribs did not. Their protest was so intense I yelped. Or screamed. Possibly wailed. Not sure—I was too busy hurting.

"*Darling*, you have to be *careful*," she said, leaning over and picking up my bag. She fumbled for my phone, somehow keeping one eye on the road and the other on my bag, and eventually managed to pull it out.

Then she answered it. "Hello?"

A pause.

"Justin, dear! How are you?" she asked in a tone so casual you'd think he hadn't been duct taped to a chair only an hour earlier.

Another pause—longer this time.

"That's good to hear. We're fine. Well, darling is a bit worse for wear, but rest assured—"

"GoneGodDammit!" I yelled and, agony or not, yanked the phone out of my mother's hand. "Justin," I said using every little trick I'd ever learned from yogis, gurus, martial artists and athletes to suppress another wail.

"Kat—you OK?"

His voice was soothing, and I forgot my pain for a second. *He's the best drug ever*, I thought (in my head, this time). Corny romantic stuff, but true nonetheless.

"I am," I said. "You?"

"I'm fine—but Kat, we've got to call the cops or the FBI or whatever. Those guys are nuts."

"No cops. Not yet."

"Why not?"

I didn't answer.

Justin answered for me. "Because there's something you're hiding and can't tell me what. Not yet, at least."

"Yeah," I said. A tear rolled down my cheek and over the fingers that held the phone. From the pain or from hearing the hurt in his voice, I wasn't sure. "But I'll tell you everything as soon as I'm back. Promise."

Justin didn't say anything back and I could tell from how he was breathing that he was holding back tears of his own.

"How are the others?" I asked, desperately trying to move the conversation away from this. My ribs hurt—but this was torture.

"They're fine," he said. "Egya took the worst of it. He kept goading them with—"

"My wonderful personality!" I heard Egya say from somewhere in the background.

"Yeah," Justin chuckled. "Mr. Personality here has two black eyes and a swollen lip ..."

His voice trailed off. I think the implication of what he was saying hit him as soon as the words came out. Egya had been hurt and hurt bad. Two black eyes meant that his nose was broken, and that wasn't something that happened without a whole lot of *ouch*. Justin was probably realizing what Egya had done for him ... put the Cherubs' focus off of him and onto Egya. He must be feeling guilt, weak for not taking the punishment himself.

"This is not your fault," I said. "If it's anyone's, it's mine."

"Don't forget me, darling," my mother chimed in.

"Oh, I haven't," I said through gritted teeth.

Turning my attention back to the phone, I said, "I'm so sorry for my part in this. I swear that when I get back, I'll tell you everything. *Everything*. And with those cards finally out on the table, you can decide whether or not you want to keep ..." I struggled for the words.

"Being an item?" Justin offered.

I laughed. That was the expression I used the first time we kissed. Him using it now meant that not all was lost.

I nodded, then felt stupid, since we were on the phone. "Being an item." I paused, thinking of the best way to say what I needed to say next. "Justin, honey," I started. "Do you mind if I speak with Egya? I really need to—"

"Sure," he said, in a hurt tone. "Since he's already seen all the cards on the table." I heard footsteps and a slammed door, and I winced.

The next voice to come on the line was Egya's. "Hi, girl," he said. "How bad is it?"

"Three, maybe four broken ribs. Justin stormed off, didn't he?"

"Ouch ... and yes. But he'll be fine. Torture can be emotional. Where are you now?"

"On the highway going somewhere my mother needs to be."

"Where? Deirdre and I can join you! You might need our muscle. Well, *her* muscle. I'm more of a roadrunner-style fighter. You know—beep, beep—push them off a cliff, that kind of stuff."

I chuckled. "Thank you, but no. I need you to protect Justin. He's not equipped."

"He's tougher than you think."

"I know. I just don't know if *Justin and I* are tougher than I think."

There was silence before Egya sighed and said, "That's not a bad thing, girl. Better to know that now than after you're barefoot, pregnant and encumbered by cooking utensils."

"Egya!" I said, and immediately regretted my outburst. I groaned in pain.

"Joke, joke. Well, partially a joke. It's better that you know he'll accept you for who you are and forgive you for who you were *now*. Later might be far more painful."

Egya was right. I hated it when Egya was right.

"OK," I said. "Then I guess almost being killed isn't all bad. It's forcing me to tell him. Yay for silver linings and all that jazz."

All that jazz. GoneGodDammit, I'd just let one of my mother's phrases slip. I could practically *hear* her smiling at me from the driver's seat.

"Yay, indeed."

"Thank you, Egya. For what you did for him. That was very brave."

"As your mother says, 'Pish posh and all that jazz.' " (Cringe … he'd caught me.) "It wasn't brave. I need a punch in the nose every now and then. It helps clean my Karmatic slate."

"Consider yourself squeaky clean," I said, peering over at my mother. If she was listening to our conversation anymore, she made no indication of it. She was lost in thought again. Something was clearly bothering her. "Egya, I've got to go."

"I know, girl. You do you, we'll be here doing us." He paused. "That sounded weird."

I laughed. "Thanks. Oh and Egya, please tell Deirdre that Captain Excellent, Van Wilder and Hannibal King were an absolutely *inspired* idea."

"Huh?"

"She'll get it," I said, ending the call. I looked over at my mother; her eyes stared off into the distance. Clearly not optimal for driving.

"Mother, thistle for your thoughts?"

It was something she used to say to me as a child. Of course, being in Scotland, she'd actually give me a thistle with the question, but since I didn't have one, I gave her knee a light squeeze.

She didn't respond, either to my word or my touch, and I was beginning to think she wouldn't when she said, "We need to get you patched up. Oh, and remember when you said you recognized that Divine Cherub hunter's voice?

"Not his voice," I said. "But I thought it was from Inverness, from our time."

She nodded, her eyes finally focusing. "Well, darling, I think you may be right."

"I'm right, huh?" I said, soaking in the rareness of being right for once. At least in my mother's eyes. "So you heard it, too?"

"Oh, more than that—I think I know who he is …"

16

KILLERS UNSUNG AND MODESTY
LOST

We drove into a rest spot. The whole drive there, despite my constant nagging, my mother refused to tell me what she knew about these Divine Cherubs, especially the one with the accent. Whatever her reasons, she promised she'd tell me everything she knew after I was patched up.

We walked into a fearsome goliath of modern innovation—the twenty-four-hour mini-mall. It had one of those mega pharmacies with enough supplies to fight the Ebola virus, where she bought gauze, medical tape and a sports bra. Why one store supplied all three, I'll never know; strangely, I missed the days when you had to literally travel to another city just to get certain supplies.

Walking up to the counter, a Mongolian eloko tended the till. He stared ahead with his giant, lower jaw tusks and hairy red cheeks. He looked like a red gorilla, and if it wasn't for the fact that he was only three feet tall, he'd be soul-crushingly frightening. At that size, he was downgraded to just terrifying and possibly a little adorable.

Not exactly the ideal customer-facing service rep, but I guess at this time of night, the only people this store could get to work here were Others. That, or they just liked how cheap Other labor was. As of yet, Other rights hadn't extended to minimum wage, and so technically you could get away with paying them peanuts. I'm not kidding ... the erewan who worked at the corner by 7-Eleven near campus was being paid in bags of peanuts until a bunch of us got him a real salary. The erewan was grateful, but being a three-headed elephant, he ended up blowing most of his salary on peanuts anyway.

The eloko rang us up and tried to give us a human-like smile, which came off more like *I want to suck your bone marrow* than *Have a nice day.*

With supplies in hand, we made our way to the bathroom.

"Strip," my mother said.

"Excuse me?"

"Or at least take off your shirt."

"What if someone comes in?" I asked, hating the childish twang that came with the question.

"Then someone comes in. At this time of night, they'll probably assume I'm your John and ask to join in."

I stared at her. "You're sick in the head."

"Your shirt." She held out her hand.

I unbuttoned my blouse—agony with every unfastened button— and handed it over. As I did, I noted the huge soot-covered foot print on the front of it. It would literally take magic to clean that.

"Oh my, darling ..." my mother said, unable to hide her concern.

Hobbling over to the mirror, I looked at my chest. A giant, bruise-colored footprint that matched the one on my blouse set deep in my skin.

"That will take weeks to fade," she said.

I nodded. Probably the only thing I missed about being a vampire was my ability to heal. OK, not the only thing. I missed my super speed, strength, heightened senses, preternatural memory—

As if reading my mind (and I *know* all those thoughts were in my head, not spoken aloud this time), my mother said, "I miss being a vampire." I had expected a question to follow—something like, *Do you miss it, too?* but my mother just fell silent.

She started to unravel the gauze and finally said, "Your bra?"

I looked at her again. "Excuse me?"

"Darling, we can't put this stuff over that lacy piece you got on. Aubade Entrevue, by the way?"

I nodded.

"Excellent taste. Justin must be very pleased."

"Mother," I said, my cheeks going DEFCON 1.

She smiled at my reaction. "Anywhooo—your bra."

I didn't move.

"You can't put this on yourself."

I groaned. She was right.

"And I am your mother. It's not like I haven't see you ... without."

Again she was right. I started to unclasp, but the pain of moving my arms that way was too much.

"Here, let me do it." She reached behind me and unclasped me one-handed. All the college guys would have been envious of her skill, I'm sure. "There you go," she said, gently guiding the straps over my arms.

Once bare, she began to wrap me. Tight. It hurt, but as soon as a half dozen rows were wrapped around me, I started to feel better. It was good not having my ribs bouncing around in my chest, poking things not meant to be poked.

"You know," she said as she started to apply the medical tape. "You inherited those from your father." She pointed at my boobs.

"Again—and I feel like I say this a lot—*excuse* me?"

"Small breasts ran in your father's family. I had hoped you'd get *my* girls, but we can't all be this lucky, I suppose." She did a little shimmy, which was amplified to a full-on rumble in this tiny room.

"I'm hardly small," I said as she helped put the sports bra on me. "I'm quite average for this era."

"You are. But average is so boring, isn't it? Or doesn't Justin think so?"

I sighed. "Help me put my blouse back on, Mother. Wouldn't want people to see how small I am and have you ashamed of your only daughter."

↔

. . .

My mother helped me back to the car and, before I could say anything, closed the door and gestured like she forgot something, jogging back toward the mall.

Alone, I watched my mother make her way back inside and wondered if she really had changed. I wanted it to be true, but was cautious to have too much hope.

But, if I'm being honest … I kind of owe her the benefit of the doubt.

OK, not kind of … I owe her a lot more than that.

↔↔↔

Old Scotland—Several Weeks After Katrina Darling Died

Most of what I remember about being a kid was being really scared. I was fifteen when I died, and even though I had all these vampiric powers, I was still a kid. I didn't understand that nothing could hurt me. That the only pain I would experience going forward was the wounds my own mind inflicted on me.

I didn't know just how powerful I was.

In those early days, I drank when I had to, trying to take as few lives as I could (and failing), and I always picked my … ah … *food* (for lack of a better term, I suppose) from the back alleys and newly released prisoners that the Highlands offered.

That was the kind of vampire I was in the early days. That would soon change, however. *I* would change—care less, kill more. My mind would harden. So would the place where my soul used to be.

But those transformations would take years.

In those early days, I cried so much that I got used to seeing the world through the prism of my own tears. I wanted to die and didn't know how. That's not true—I knew how I died, I just didn't know how I could die *again*, in this form. And never come back.

As I wandered the Highlands, contemplating death, I played the circumstances of my infection over and over again. Thanks to my father, I didn't have a sire vampire to teach me what my powers were or how to use them. There were no books or movies to teach me ... there was only legend; and me being so young, my parents had protected me from fearing those that go bump in the night.

So I had to learn everything about my nature on my own. And in my naïveté, a single thought ran through my head.

If I was turned by the bite of a vampire ... can I turn another with a bite of my own?

The idea consumed me, my head swimming with the possibility that I could sire other vampires. And as soon as that thought entered my head, it was quickly followed by the tempting thought that I didn't need to be alone.

In my eagerness to have the family I lost, I decided to test this theory on my mother—partly because I figured she would be easier prey (after all, my father had fought off a vampire on his own), but mostly because I loved my father dearly and the thought of accidently killing him was more than I could bear.

I loved my mother—but she was someone I was willing to lose in my quest *not* to be alone. And those three words never quite stopped ringing in my head.

Cast ... her ... out.

↔

I staked out my family's cabin on the hill, watching my father's comings and goings. It took a few weeks to assess the pattern, but eventually it became obvious: when he went out riding alone, he would always return in an hour or so; but when he went to the barn and both he and the farm hand went out together—he would be gone for hours. No idea what they did, but I assumed they went to the pub. The farm hand was an unsavory character with a scar over his eye who had been giving me creepy looks for the last few years of my life. As far as I was concerned, I could kill him too, but he wasn't the mission.

I waited for a night that both my father and the farm hand left, then made my entrance.

By this point, I was beginning to feel comfortable with my powers and, in my childish arrogance, did not hide my approach. As I drew nearer, I even began singing a song my mother frequently sang to me as a child when she was in a playful mood.

"One, two, three aleerie ..."

I approached the cabin.

"Four, five, six aleerie ..."

She looked outside and, seeing me, quickly closed the windows. I could hear her boarding up the house. It didn't bother me.

"Seven, eight, nine aleerie ..."

I reached the door and smashed it open with one powerful blow. She was hiding in the corner, a kitchen knife in her hand. I smirked.

"Ten aleerie overball ..."

When I was a living child, she tickled me every time the word *aleerie* was sung.

"One, two, three aleerie ..."

I did more than tickle her with that last *aleerie*. I drained her until just before the moment her heart stopped. Then I withdrew and, holding her in my arms, sung the rest of the song as the vampire virus took hold.

"I saw Mrs. Peerie sittin' on her bumbaleerie, eatin' chocolate biscuits ..."

↔

Transformations, I came to understand, were instant. Why my transformation took so long, I may never know. I never met my sire, nor understood the conditions of my bite. As far as I know, I'm the only vampire that has ever taken more than a hour to change. There was a chunk of time during the twentieth century in which I became obsessed with interviewing vampires to learn if I was really alone in that respect. I'm pretty sure Ann Rice got her book idea from me.

That night, my mother turned, became a newborn vampire, and left with me. The next day I returned to our cabin and called for my father, offering him the gift of the vampire's bite as well. Offering him his family back. For eternity.

He refused me.

Us.

And when I realized that transforming my mother would not force my father's hand, I abandoned my mother to figure out how to be a vampire on her own.

Our paths often crossed … and more often than meeting her, I came to learn that my mother embraced her vampiric nature fully. Her legend preceded her.

Mine … I rarely met a vampire, or any other kind of creature for that matter, who'd heard of Katrina Darling.

Such is life. And death.

Such is the mother's way.

17

CODEINE, KILLERS NOW SUNG
AND BLESSED SLEEP

"*Y*oohoo!" my mother shouted from the mall entrance. She had a couple of those orange pill bottles in her hand, and even though she was across the parking lot, I could hear the pills rattle.

Getting in the driver's side, she tossed me the two bottles and said, "Take two of each."

"What are they?"

"Codeine and a mild sleeping pill, darling. You need something to help you manage the pain."

"I'm managing just fine." Although, truth be told, there was only so much breathing could do for me. Especially in a bouncing car.

"Stubborn as a mule. Just like your father. Take the pills. Trust me."

"I would, except I'm pretty sure you need a prescription—for the codeine, at least. How did you get these? Not the old-fashioned way ..." I was referring to her *feminine wiles*, of course. But given we were both ex-vampires, the old-fashioned way could mean *killing the pharmacist*.

She rolled her eyes and then gave me a wry smile. "Yes, the old-fashioned way," she said.

"What? You ... you know—" I made a very suggestive gesture.

"Darling, mind your manners, and no—nothing so vulgar. I just batted my eyelashes, told him I forgot my prescription, promised to call in with all the information if he would only save me a trip back to this hellhole. I also promised that the call would be accompanied with a location where he could buy me a beer."

"So, let me get this straight … you got the medication by insinuating he could take you on a date?"

My mother nodded. "See the doors that 'above average' opens?"

I chuckled and then winced.

"Come on, darling," she said. "Two of each." I hesitated—more because I was in pain than for any other reason—and my mother interpreted my pause as further resistance. "OK," she sighed, "I'll make you a deal. Pop two of each and I'll tell you who I think the Divine Cherub with the sexy accent is."

Her last words hung in the air like a worm on a hook. I'm sure there were plenty of fish that knew what they were getting into when they took the bait but didn't care. Sometimes a wiggle is just too much to resist.

I took two of each.

My mother gave me a distrusting look, so I opened my mouth wide, lifted my tongue and let out a muffled, "Satisfied?"

She beamed. "Ravished."

↔

By the GoneGods, those pills were *strong*. Within minutes my ribs stopped hurting and my head started swimming in La La Land. I was still present enough to know that my ribs were still very much broken, but I didn't care. Hell, I wouldn't have cared if every nerve in my body had been connected directly into a NutriBullet. I'd just smoothie them up and slurp it down.

"Darling," my mother said. "Are you listening?"

I nodded.

She took a deep breath and said, "Remember that farm hand father employed all those years ago? The one with the scar on his eye? I think he's back."

"How?" I muttered. If I wasn't so out of it, I would have known the answer immediately.

"I turned him," she said.

"And he's back to … what?"

"You remember how loyal he was to your father? He probably wants to get me back for what happened to him. Not," she quickly added, lifting a finger in my direction, "that I had anything to do with your father's demise. I left him well alone after I was turned. I just wanted you to know that."

A serious look of concern washed over my mother's face. She really didn't have anything to do with my father's death and wanted to make damn sure that I knew it, too. I could almost hear Mergen smacking his lips on the Truth. So I believed her, which seemed to bring her relief. I guess she figured that if I thought she was responsible for him turning to dust, that no amount of change in this or any other world would stop me from going after her.

But I knew that she was innocent without her saying a word.

I knew because *I* killed him.

Wait—did I think that or say it out loud or just *thought* I thought it? Or said it. Or … whatever.

Damn—these drugs were intense.

"OK," I finally managed to say, "so that's what the big secret is? You turned the farm hand—"

"Simione."

"Simione—and didn't want to tell me?"

"Well … it was just that your father was still alive when I did it, so it kind of felt like I was cheating on him."

"By not biting Father?"

"By not turning him. I often pondered what life would be like if I had turned him. The three of us might be together again, in this era, and finally become the family we were meant to be."

I shrugged. "Maybe. But then again—three hundred years together might cause … friction."

"You mean like it is for us."

I nodded.

Now it was my mother's turn to shrug. "Perhaps, but your father was always the one who kept the peace between us. I suspect that if he was still around, he'd resume his role of peacekeeper."

"More like *barrier*," I said, giggling, though it wasn't that funny. Egya would be disappointed in me.

"Barrier, peacekeeper—point is, maybe if he was here we wouldn't be fighting."

"Maybe," I said, putting my hand on her shoulder. "Maybe."

↔

As nice as our little chat was, eventually the drugs got to be too much and I began to drift off into dreamless sleep. When I woke, I saw from the clock on the dashboard that it was early afternoon. I had been sleeping for almost ten hours. I lifted my head—a lot more effort given that my chest still blazed like the flames of Tartarus—and saw that we were parked on some country road.

"Where are we?" I asked my mother, who was using the rearview mirror to apply makeup.

"Where do you think?"

"At Lizile's?"

"Bingo! Score one for the detective."

"Snarky much? Wake up on the wrong side of the car?"

My mother sighed. "Sorry, darling. It's just that I'm so close to finding the amulet and completing my mission … I guess I'm just nervous."

"So go. She was only six hours away. You must have gotten here hours ago."

"Go in without *you*, darling? I could *never*."

"Mother—that amulet is *your* mission. Not mine."

"True—but today is 'take your daughter to work' day. Swallow these." She had two codeines in her hand. "And let's go say hello."

18

TWINS, AMULETS, ALCHEMY AND "WHAT DID YOU SAY ...?"

*W*e walked up to an old cabin in the middle of a heavily wooded area. To call this place "secluded" would be to say that tourists occasionally visit Times Square. This cabin was practically on another planet.

But an ex-vampire living in the middle of nowhere wasn't a surprise. Many of our kind chose to live as far away from people as they could get. Some did it because they felt intense guilt over all the death and carnage they caused way back when. Some hid themselves because a very significant part of them missed being a vampire—and they couldn't stand that the desire for blood and death and carnage was still a part of them. And still others chose seclusion because after centuries of eating people, you kind of stopped liking them. Out here you didn't need to deal with a single human soul ... which sounded appealing. Even to me.

Perhaps the main reason for seclusion, for both vampires and really any other Other, was that we don't belong. I'm not saying it's like we get all mopey and can't relate to anyone ... I'm talking about, in this new GoneGod world, the hatred and prejudice and vitriol many Others have to face every single day. There comes a point where that just becomes too much to handle, and it's either burn all your time and kill yourself, or build a kickass cabin in the woods.

I supposed there were many other reasons they hid—each to their own—but what all ex-vampires had in common was that they also blocked out the light as best they could.

This cabin practically didn't have walls. Sure, the trees created a natural canopy, but that wasn't enough to block sunlight from getting through the massive sliding doors on the eastern entrance, or the massive bay windows that were situated on the west ... and seeing this beautiful cabin, I wondered two things: one—did an ex-vampire really live here? and two (and what I really wanted to know)—how the hell did she manage to build this, here?

I suspected I would get an answer to at least one of those questions. Probably not the one I wanted, but by hook or crook, we'd know if a vampire lived here soon enough.

↔

The windows told us immediately that no one was home. Or if they were, they were hiding in one of the pieces of furniture, be it the two-seater couch or single mattress that sat on the floor. Talk about a stoic vamp ... not your typical ex-creature of the night. We tended to like our creature comforts.

"Are you sure we got the right place?"

My mother held up her phone, looking for a signal. "I think so. I'd tell you for sure, but ..."

"Should we go in?" I asked, tugging at the sliding door. It held shut. In fact, it held *too* shut. Usually a sliding door would jiggle or rattle under any kind of pressure. This one was solid, as if it were a solid wall.

I tugged harder. Same effect—as in *no* effect.

I put a hand up to the glass, cutting out as much glare as I could, and looked inside. One couch, one mattress, a couple frying pans and hearth off to one side. For such a beautiful and painstakingly created exterior, this ex-vampire did very little for the interior. Something wasn't right.

"Mother," I said quietly, "what line of alchemy did the twins practice?"

"Containment, mostly. Some potion work and—"

She cut herself off as a thought occurred to her. Then, bending down, she dug around for a rock that she promptly—and without warning—threw at the window I was standing next to.

I expected the glass to shatter. But instead of a crash, I heard a *thud* as the stone bounced off the window and hit my head.

"Illusions," my mother said.

"Ow," I said.

↔

So the window was an illusion, which meant that what we saw inside was also an illusion. To power such a grand glamor must take a lot of magic, which in turn meant burning a lot of time.

But vampires—well, *ex*-vampires—were human now, which meant no more magic, the time-burning variety or no. Not that we had much magic when we were in full-fang mode. We just had abilities that were *granted* to us by magic. Sadly, those abilities didn't include flying, fireballs or any other kinds of cantrips or spells.

Which meant that this couldn't be Lizile's place. This belonged to some Other who was willing to burn a heck of a lot of time to stay hidden. The Other's magic wouldn't have to be ongoing, either. They would set it up to turn on only when they needed to be hidden and for as short a period of time as possible.

Every second we stood here, the creature inside literally aged by—what?—hours, days, maybe more? We needed to leave before that poor being turned itself to dust.

"Mother, this can't be Lizile's place."

From the slow nod my mother gave me, she agreed. Evidently she'd come to the same conclusions as me. But unlike me, she hadn't decided it was time to leave.

Instead she called out, "Yoohoo! We know you're in there and we mean you no harm. We're here to say hello. Stop wasting your time for no reason."

Nothing happened.

"Come on, Mother. Whoever is inside doesn't want to talk to us," I said, touching her elbow in a gesture that we should go.

She jerked it away a bit too harshly for my gentle plea, causing needles of pain to go through my chest. Either she didn't realize she had hurt me or didn't care—either way, she called out, "Let's avoid the 'big bad wolf' scenario, shall we? I fear my huffing and puffing days are over. I'm more into burning now." She pulled out a menthol and lit it to illustrate her point. "Don't make me siphon some gas from my car and set this place on fire. It's a hybrid. Gas is precious for that damn thing."

I turned to face my mother and saw the old crazed gleam in her eyes when she was getting ready to do something particularly vicious.

"Mother, what's gotten into you?" I hissed.

"Darling," she said, not taking her eyes off of the cabin, "my intel is good. Very good. She is in there and no glamor on this plane or any other will stop me from completing my mission."

"But your mission *is* complete," I said. "We have half the amulet. No one can use it for ill or good." This was a thought I had had before, but didn't say it to her mostly because I wanted to know more about the amulet and what her mission really was. *Curiosity—thy name is Kat.*

My mother glanced at me dismissively. "My mission was to get the whole thing. After all, the good guys might need it one day."

"But—"

"But *nothing*—I am here for a reason," she said, loud enough that anyone listening—say, behind a glamor—would hear, "and I will not be dissuaded. Lizile, my name is Charlotte Darling ... perhaps you have heard of me? Of course you have. Well, then, you know enough that I will not leave, not until—"

The sliding door opened—but not in the way sliding doors should. Rather, a *hinged* door swung out and a tall, sylph-like woman walked to the threshold. She had "vampire" written all over her—a long, purple satin skirt, a white long-sleeve blouse under a black and red corset and deepset sage green eyes. But perhaps the most telling sign was that she did not step into the sunlight, careful to stay out of the rays' path.

Lizile gestured for us to enter.

We did, and as I approached the door I saw that the glamor remained. On the outside, it looked like a pane of glass that showed a spacey, sparsely furnished interior. But the inside of the door was heavy oak with steel bars that were intended to keep unwanted guests locked out.

And anyone who entered, imprisoned inside.

19

WHO'S YOUR DECORATOR?

Once inside, I found myself in an interior that was much more aligned with what I knew of vampires: heavy Persian rugs covering the floor, sometimes stacked three deep; tapestries from China and Japan covered the walls; and antiques of unimaginable value sat on every mahogany table, side-table and coffee-table. In other words, for the hosts of the *Antiques Roadshow* this place was the stuff of wet dreams.

And pretty typical for us. My castle (small one, nothing too fancy) back in Scotland was similarly decorated, although I was more of an oak gal.

What wasn't typical were the shelves that lined the back wall. Spanning about twenty feet wide and easily fifteen feet high, they were filled with jar after jar of liquids and powders, herbs and other stuff you might expect to find in a witch's lair.

"Nice place," I said.

"Nice glamor," my mother added. "Must have cost you a lot of time. Or a lot of some Other's time …?"

Lizile didn't take the bait. She tilted her head from side to side before saying in a voice that sounded more like a clock than words,

"Not time. Resources. This house was made like this before the magic left us. I use my science to sustain." She gestured at her shelves.

"Science," I said. "Don't you mean alchemy?"

The old vampire gave me a wry smile, and I almost expected to see fangs poking out; this ex-vamp was still very much oozing the vampire's aura. "Magic is only science unexplained. And alchemy is science not understood. I mean what I mean, girl."

My mother tapped me on the shoulder in an admonishing manner. "Don't be rude. *Girl.*"

Her words didn't hurt. But even the light, almost playful tap hurt my ribs.

Lizile saw me wince. "You are hurt."

"Cracked ribs and—"

"It's nothing," my mother interjected. "Let us get down to business. We need something you have."

Lizile ignored my mother, continuing to gaze at me with unblinking eyes. Then, without a word, she glided—well, walked, but her legs hardly moved under that long, satin skirt, causing a graceful yet unsettling gliding effect—over to her shelf and pulled down a vial of ... something.

"Here—drink. It will not heal you, nor will it take away the pain. It will, however, shorten the time needed for the former, and lessen the intensity of the latter."

She corked it open and a purplish mist that screamed "magic potion cliché" tumbled out.

"Ahhh," I said looking at my mother.

She nodded. "Go ahead. Lizile knows that hurting my daughter will cost her."

At this, Lizile nodded in agreement, still never taking her unblinking eyes off of me.

I sipped it, expecting to taste something between black bananas and algae. But what touched my tongue tasted more like ... like ...

"Is that ... cinnamon?"

"And nutmeg."

"Humph, who knew a witch's brew was so tasty?" I downed the rest in two quick gulps.

"I prefer 'alchemist potion.'"

I smacked my lips. Even though I had literally *just* ingested it, I did feel much better already. Don't get me wrong—my ribs still hurt quite a bit. But the pressure felt less intense and it was easier to breathe.

"We're here for the Amulet of Souol. Well, *your* half of it," my mother said, clearly impatient by this little display.

Amulet of Souol, I thought. Mother was holding out on me.

"I know," Lizile said.

"You do?" Mother sounded genuinely surprised, which gave me a genuine taste of satisfaction.

"Of course, Charlotte Darling—your legend proceeds you, and a vampire of your ilk would only come to this secluded place for one purpose."

"Really?" My mother lifted a dubious eyebrow.

Lizile's lips curled upward as she pointed at a telephone that probably once stood in a phone booth—once, as in the 1950s. "Dostarious called me."

"Really?" my mother said again. "I thought you two weren't speaking."

Lizile lifted a lecturing finger. "Not seeing each other. Different than not speaking. We are still scientists, after all. We still have notes that need comparing, experiments that require peer rev—"

"The amulet?" my mother cut in, her hand out.

"*Now* who's being rude?" I said, glaring at my mother.

"I do apologize, darling, but it has been a long night and there is much still to do."

"Indeed," Lizile agreed.

This surprised me, as I half expected her to be insulted by my mother's taciturn positioning and kick us out. Well, she could try at least. I very much doubted my mother would leave without a fight.

"There is much to do. Tell me, Charlotte Darling—why should I give you the amulet?"

"Because my organization will protect *it*." My mother hit the word "it" hard, and I got the sneaking suspicion she wasn't talking about the amulet.

"Protect it?"

"Yes ... with our lives."

"*Use* it."

"If we can."

"You can't. Dostarious and I have tried. It is beyond the knowledge of anyone but the truly divine."

"Hold on," I cut in, turning to my mother. "I thought you said the amulet answered your greatest question."

"It does, darling," my mother said. "Now shush."

Lizile nodded.

"So what's all this cryptic shit of *beyond the knowledge* and *protect it?*"

Lizile leveled a raised eyebrow at my mother. "She does not know?"

My mother gave Lizile a deadly look and said, "She knows enough."

"Indeed." Lizile returned her unblinking gaze to me. "Your mother tells the truth ... the amulet will answer its owner one and only one question. Oft, it is not the question asked, but rather the question that hides in the heart of those who ask. Many a fool have wasted its use by filling their heart with a meaningless or temporal query."

Now it was my turn to lift an eyebrow. "Can I have an example?"

" 'Dost he love me?' " she spat. "Love is fleeting, it changes. The amulet may answer yes, for today he does, only to be wrong tomorrow when he does not. I wasted my question by asking 'Can lead be turned to gold?' when I should have asked, '*How* is lead turned to gold?' Do you understand now?"

"Yes," I said.

"So the bearer must be prepared—must meditate on their question, mold it in their heart, pursue it with every fiber of their being. This is why your mother is the perfect one to ask—"

"Enough," my mother interjected. "Do not presume what my question would be. Nor presume that I intend to ask it a question at all."

I looked over at my mother and saw an immutable sternness I hadn't seen since I was a child.

"My apologizes," Lizile said. "I shall give you my half of the Amulet of Souol. But only in exchange for something I desire." As she spoke she continued with her unwavering gaze at me.

I was beginning to get nervous.

Finally she said: "That your daughter and I have a few minutes together, alone."

Why? I thought. If it was for a staring contest, I was a goner. But a part of me knew it would be something much more sinister, and I was probably a goner anyway.

20

NO STARING CONTEST, NO QUESTIONS, NO FUTURE

*L*izile persuaded my mother to not only leave us alone for a few minutes, but also to give up her half of the Amulet of Souol. There were a few rules my mother put in place, which mostly revolved around Lizile staying out of our relationship. Clearly Lizile believed my mother had a question she wished to ask—and even more clearly my mother didn't want me to know what that question might be.

Note to self: ask my Psych prof, what is the technical term for "micro-managing, control-freak, nut-job"?

I half expected the strange former vampire to protest, but she just nodded, gave her half of the amulet to my mother without so much as a second thought and led me into a back room, gesturing for me to sit on an old cigar chair with cracking leather.

I sat and she gestured to see my hand. I thought she was going to read my palm or some crap like that, but with a speed I did not think possible for humans, she pricked my finger with her hair pin and collected a drop of my blood on a piece of glass.

I pulled away, sucking my finger. The taste of blood still repulsed me, after all these years. "What the hell?"

"Shush, girl. It is only a drop of blood. I wish to share knowledge, but knowledge should only be shared with those deserving of it. I must see your mettle, first," she said, then, standing, she pulled out an old microscope I think I once saw at an apothecary's lab in pre-Industrial Age London. She placed the glass under the microscope's lens, adjusting its focus before smiling and looking up at me again.

"By the GoneGods ... my brother was right."

"About what? What did you see?"

Lizile ignored my question with a question of her own. "Do you know how to imbue an item with magic?"

I shook my head. "I've never really thought about it. I guess divine creatures transfer some of their magic into the item, right?"

"Really? Do you think a god would ever imbue this place with magic?" She waved her hand, drawing attention to our surroundings in a dismissive gesture, as if acknowledging that her place was less than pretty. Less than magical. So she was a self-aware vampire. How rare.

"So how do you keep the glamor going? You're not an Other. You don't have magic. When we entered, you mentioned something about depleting your resources ...?"

"Significance. I long ago learned how to imbue a place or object with *significance*. Something easily done before the gods left, and perhaps by instinct or dumb luck, I managed to imbed this secluded cabin with much *significance* after they had left."

"Significance?" I repeated.

"Yes. Significance."

"Forgive me, but what is the significance of *significance*?"

She sighed, not hiding her disappointment in my lack of under-standing (she was beginning to remind me of my Psych prof) and said, "Even the most powerful amongst the newly made mortals cannot *give* their magic to someone or something. Only a god can ... it is one of the traits that makes them gods and not simply powerful Others.

"No, items become magical because of *significance*. Take this amulet, for example ... it is over seven thousand years old, its first owner the Pharaoh of Narmer. Every night the Pharaoh would ask the amulet a question, placing it erect on the palace shrine. Then he would wait for the sun to rise. If the sun pierced the amulet's center, casting a shadow on the Key of Life, he took it as an omen meaning 'Yes.' If the first shadow cast was partial or not at all, then the answer was 'No.' " She chuckled. "In other words, the answers 'Yes' and 'No' solely depended on how cloudy the morning was."

Worse than a Magic 8-Ball, I thought. *You'd think he'd eventually clue in.*

"Indeed," she agreed to my out-loud thought. "He might have, but he placed so much *significance* on this ritual that in time—and much shorter than you'd expect—the amulet *did* start to answer his questions. And his children's questions. More and more asked, prescribing more and more rules as to how to ask, and eventually we got this item before us. An amulet imbued with thousands of years of significance, and rules as to how to ask. Do you understand?"

I nodded. "Magic by mistake. No miracle required."

She smiled. "So many items possess both minor and major magical properties. In fact, it was this very process that created the very first vampire."

That caught my attention. "How so?"

"Have you heard of the Rooh Ina'ah? The Soul Jar?"

I shook my head.

She gave me an admonishing look. "You were never curious where your soul went when you were turned?"

"Heaven?" I said, with a bit of cheek thrown in to mask my indignity.

"More like limbo. Legend says that there is a jar—more of an urn, really—that holds the souls of all those turned. Vampires, werewolves. Everything infected. When the gods left, it is said that the urn was destroyed, thus letting our souls return to us."

I thought about this. A jar that held our souls. I had always assumed that our souls went away, but never thought about where or how. It made sense that they would need a place to go, and I guess I had hoped it was a pleasant place. Seems that our souls weren't so lucky. A jar. Or urn. Whatever. That sat on some shelf somewhere on Earth, abandoned.

"Interesting legend … but is it true?"

"We don't know," she said.

"OK," I said, getting a bit bored of this cryptic, *Look at me, I'm a scary vampire* routine. "Why are you telling me this?"

"Promise me that you will not ask the Amulet of Souol a question until you are ready."

"Ready for what?"

"To embrace your destiny."

"What are you talking about?"

"*Promise* me," she said so forcefully that I actually jumped in my chair. Not my proudest moment.

"OK, OK, I promise. Not that I understand what I *am* promising, but I promise."

"Good," she said, calming down. She handed me the glass plate that had my blood on it. "Destiny is held in blood … and your blood tells me that your destiny will be full of …" She searched for the words. "… *choices* and *questions*. I do not know what your fate will be, but I can tell you this … you will play a *significant* role in the war that is to come."

I gulped, forgetting to breathe. "What war?"

"The war that will end everything."

21

GOODBYES, CAR RIDES AND CRASHES

We left the strange alchemist vampire's lair in silence, me clutching my glass slide of blood, both lost in our own thoughts. My thoughts went to everything that was messed up in my life. My boyfriend didn't know who I was ... and once he found out, he was going to leave me. My friends (boyfriend included) were hiding, afraid that the Divine Cherubs—the leader of whom used to leer at me while working for my father—would come after them ... again, because of me. Some strange, possibly insane ex-vampire thought I was going to be instrumental for some upcoming war ... but how? I was barely instrumental in managing my own laundry!

But I've met enough weird ancient creatures to know that you never dismiss their comments out of hand—no matter how nonsensical they may sound.

And if that wasn't enough—I was failing Psychology 101.

OK, that last one wasn't true. I could very well fail, but not until I didn't pass Tuesday's test. Of course, I'd need to show up first, and given the direction my mother was driving now, even *that* wasn't a given.

I looked over at my mother as she held the steering wheel at 10 and 2. She stared ahead, but I knew enough about how she operated to know that the road was the last thing on her mind. I wasn't sure what my mother was thinking about—I guessed it was about the amulet. She needed to finish her *mission*. But I hoped she was also thinking about me and the lie—or, rather, omission of truth—that hung between us. She wasn't telling me something, and it was obviously weighing on her. Whatever it was, it was going to piss me off. She knew it and now I knew it, too. But she also knew that not telling me would piss me off even more.

I reached into her purse and pulled out the amulet, putting it in my bag. If she wanted it back, she'd have to convince me to give it to her. Or fight me for it. Both were bad options, but given how banged up I was, fighting me might be the path of least resistance. And my mother was the "least resistance" kind of gal. But my mother didn't even react to me taking the amulet. She just kept staring ahead. Part of me wondered if she even noticed.

I briefly considered that she was suffering from depersonalization disorder or anxiety-caused detachment—and that thought was immediately followed by my utter surprise for knowing those terms. Maybe I would pass my test, after all!

I shook away those thoughts—that would have to wait for Tuesday —and focused on my mother.

Still, so much had changed. For one thing, she saved me—twice. For another, she spoke of the "right" thing, and about saving people, and she lamented about how hard it was to be human. She even drove a Prius. Vampires were generally into the big, loud and pollution monsters … which didn't make sense. If global warming was going to kill us all in a few thousand (hundred?) years, and you lived forever, you'd think the green movement would be *led* by vampires.

So either mother was changing or this was the greatest performance since the "I'm mad as hell" speech by Howard Beale in the movie Network (a little early for me—I'm more of a 1980s movie gal —but still a great film). Looking over at my distracted mother, I guessed it was a bit of both.

I also guessed that if either of us were going to get past any of this, now was the best time to get into it. But how did I start?

Then something my mother once said struck me.

What was the shortest distance between two points?

The truth, I thought.

"Excuse me, darling?" my mother asked, not taking her eyes off the road.

"Mother, there is so much you're not telling me that I find it hard to believe anything you say," I said.

Shortest distance isn't necessarily the easiest.

"Like what, darling?" my mother said, her voice now a challenging tone, her attention more on me.

"Like why you really want to get the whole amulet. Lizile alluded to something that you clearly didn't want me to know."

My mother bit her lower lip.

"Well?"

"It's complicated, darling."

"Try me. We have time."

My mother looked at me, her eyes surprisingly tearing up. "I just want us to be a family again. You and me."

But I didn't let her tears stop me. I charged on. "So stop lying and tell me what the hell is going on!"

This time a tear actually fell down her cheek. "I … I can't. I need more time to figure out how to tell you. You get that, don't you? You understand why I can't tell you now."

Those words, *I can't tell you now*, caused me so much frustration that I contemplated opening the car door and rolling out. I might have, too, had it not been for my aching ribcage.

That … and Justin.

I suddenly knew how the poor boy felt. I was always saying *"Not now." "When the timing is right."*

"Later."

"Soon."

"Eventually."

I did it because I thought it was the right thing to do, but really it was the selfish thing to do. The cowardly thing to do. I wanted him to react in a certain way and was terrified he wouldn't. Putting it off was my way to delay the rejection I was sure he was going to throw my way.

Given that I had more of my mother's personality in me than I cared to admit, I knew that she was feeling the same way. Like mother like freaking daughter. She had a secret that she feared would make me walk away from her. Abandon her. And (given our history) try to kill her.

She was scared, and that was why she held back.

OK, I could wait—for a little bit longer at least. I'd need to know before I let her run off with the amulet, but I wouldn't press her to tell me until that moment came.

"Fine," I said, "later. But know that later will be sooner than you think."

She nodded, tapping her head as she drove. "Formulating the narrative as we speak."

"A bullshit-free narrative."

"A bullshit-*light* narrative."

I managed a small laugh. "Good enough. But there's more. What about Simione? You say it's him, but how could it be? The people we fought were super strong. Simione would be a human now. There's no way he could throw us around like that. Old Inverness accent or not."

My mother sighed. Then, pulling over at a rest stop that amounted to a gas station with two pumps and an empty parking lot big enough to accommodate two hundred cars, she put the car in Park and said, "You're right. But it's not just the accent. It's what he said when he was bearing down on you with his boot. *The god of peace will soon crush Satan under your shoe.*"

"Romans?" I asked. "And isn't it 'feet'?"

My mother shrugged. She wasn't one for memorizing things unless it was the Bluefly website. "Wherever it's from, darling, that was exactly what he said to me when I ..." She closed her mouth.

"When you *what*, Mother?"

"When I buried him."

↔

"You *what?*"

"You have to understand that he and his buddies burned down my home, darling. I was *angry*. And you know what I'm like when I'm angry."

"Mom, you sound like the Hulk."

She glared at me. "You know what I mean, darling. I don't make the best decisions and I ... ahhh ... I kind of turned him into a vampire and then ... well, I didn't bury him, per se ..."

"Oh good," I said, relieved.

"I locked him in a coffin and threw him into a lake. Loch Ness, to be exact."

Holy guacamole—my mother was one vindictive bitch. "All three of them?"

"Oh no, darling, just him. I am a monster, but I do have my limits. I killed his two friends, stripped them of their masks, and put them in his coffin to ... you know, keep him company."

"Ahhh!" I screamed. "I can't believe what I'm hearing! You literally trapped an immortal being at the bottom of the lake with the dismembered body parts of his friends ... for *arson*."

"I liked that house."

"Great, Mom. Thanks for this. He kidnapped my friends, you know. And broke a few of your daughter's ribs."

"I'm not proud of it, darling. We all make mistakes."

That last sentence hit me hard. I couldn't be certain she had said it on purpose, but it brought a wave of memories back, from my darker days as a vampire. I'd done horrific things, some of which I did for no reason at all other than my being bored with eternity.

But I shoved those thoughts away. "And now he's, what? Back to get revenge?"

"I assume so. And it does explain his accent. Three hundred years of *not* hearing others speak would preserve the old Scottish twang, don't you think?"

"Not to mention *stoke the fires of hatred*. I hate to say this, Mother, but I'm kind of on his side. I'd want you dead, too."

"I know, darling, you've made that very clear in the past. But you know what it was like back when you were newly made. All these powers. No consequences. I was relishing in my newly made immortality and thought I was above things like morality."

"And decency. And any sense of mercy."

"Yes, yes," she said, waving my words away. "All of that."

And then she did the last thing I ever expected her to do.

She started crying.

↔

She turned her face away from me as heavy tears rolled down her face. I didn't know what to do. We weren't exactly the hugging type.

Well, that wasn't entirely true. We *were* the hugging type. When we were human, the first time. But that was a long time ago and the three hundred years between being human then and being human now had changed us. Both of us.

But it didn't have to, I thought. Some things could change back. All it took was that first step.

So I leaned over and gave her an awkward hug. Given that I was leaning over the Prius's gearbox, I did a pretty good job.

She touched my hand and with tear-laden eyes said, "I just want to go back to the way it was. I hate who I've become. Who I am. I want things to just return to normal. Do you think that will ever be possible?"

"In time," I said, tightening my hug.

Here was a woman struggling to be human again … just like me. Hell, in the four years that I'd been human again, I spent three of them locked away in a castle and one of them being the most awkward freshman on campus. Being human was hard, but as I hugged my mother, I realized it didn't need to be lonely.

"In time," I repeated. "We just need to find our way. And that's something we can do—"

I was going to say *together*, except we were rudely interrupted by a Dodge Ram that chose that moment to crash into the back of our parked car. Luckily my mother hadn't turned the ignition off, so the airbags deployed.

Dazed, I looked through the rearview mirror and saw a Cherub's face behind the driver's seat.

PART IV
INTERMISSION

Sitting at the bottom of a lake, Simione wonders why he hasn't drowned yet. No matter how much water he takes into his lungs, he lives on. Well, if you can call being trapped in a coffin at the bottom of the lake *living*. If you can call being an immortal *vampire* living, for that matter. But that word is one he is unwilling to consciously admit to himself. *Vampire*. As a Divine Cherub, he'd once vowed to put an end to such an abhorrence. So how can he admit to himself the truth now? That Charlotte Darling had turned him into the one thing in this world he hates most, only moments before plunging him to his eternal watery grave?

Days pass and he wonders why he doesn't die of hunger. Or the cold. Or anything else except thirst. Water is the only thing he has plenty of … enough to drown a thousand times over. But he doesn't die. He keeps living on and on and on. (He secretly knows why, but he will not let that word enter his mind—*vampire*.)

He wears his Cherub mask for the first decade, but in time the leather straps mold away and he manages to shake it off. He hoped that the same would be true of his chains, but they have only rusted, never giving up their strength so that he could break free of those as well.

During the second decade, he goes a bit mad, talking to the masks that rest in the coffin with him. They once belonged to his friends, after all. Though what remains of his friends rotted away beside him years ago.

He and his mask friends mostly reminisce about the good old days. The hunting days. When they were alive. It does sometimes disturb Simione that no bubbles emerge from him as he speaks, but hey—no bubbles had been emerging from his mask friends, either, yet he can hear them crystal clear in his head.

During the third decade, as barnacles begin to grow on his skin, he stops talking, his mind churning one single thought until it's polished to a shimmering sparkle. The thought details everything he plans to do to Charlotte Darling when he escapes.

IF you escape, one of the masks says to him.

He doesn't gratify it with a response.

Perhaps this moment is the downfall for poor ol' Simione's mind. For the thought, although completely justified, more than occupies him. It infects him. Possesses him.

And, in time, *becomes* him.

↔

This continues for yet more years, although how many, he can never say. Then one day, as if by a miracle, he hears a voice other than his own (and he admitted to himself years ago that the masks never actually spoke to him, so this comes as a particular surprise).

The voice says in a very clear and familiar Scottish accent, "Thank you for believing in us, but it's not enough. We're leaving. Good luck."

He isn't sure who "us" are, but before he can contemplate this further, he feels something grip his chest.

And he begins, finally, to drown.

After years of *not* drowning, the sensation is as unexpected as being struck by lightning in the dead of night. He squirms, desperate to find oxygen to fill his newly alive lungs. There is none—and as the world starts to fade to black, he feels something heavy and monstrous strike his coffin.

Not just strike it—tear it apart.

The old oak coffin rips asunder and the chains that once anchored him slide free. Instinctively knowing that air is up, Simione begins to swim, barely taking note of the giant whale with a very long neck and four dorsal fins that accidently saved him by striking his coffin in its own panic.

Of course, later, Simione will come back to thank Nessie for saving him. But for now, air is of utmost importance.

2 2

CAR PARKS, AIRBAGS AND SUPER HUMANS

*Y*ou learn something new every day. Today, it seemed, I was learning *many* somethings new. Currently, I was learning:

Airbags hurt.

It was like getting punched by a giant's boxing glove. My whole body got a piece of the impact and, sports bra and witch's brew or not, my ribs rattled in such a way that made me black out for the rest of the crash.

My first sense as I regained consciousness was my mother, with her healthy ribs, moaning. I opened my eyes just in time to see her get out of the car and run.

Thanks, Mom, I thought as I tried moving—far too slowly, given what was waiting for me outside.

Grabbing my bag, I crawled out of the passenger side door. I was greeted by the smallest of the three Cherubs.

So be it, I thought as I fumbled with my bag and put on my father's mask.

Then, unsheathing my dirk, I stood and said, "No quarter asked."

Might as well go out a badass, right?

The guy tilted his head in confusion. He'd obviously never been in a duel to the death before.

"You're supposed to say, 'No quarter given.' "

"Oh," he said, pulling out his telescopic nightstick. "Yeah. That."

↔

I may have been hurt, but I was far from helpless.

He lunged at me, making the classic mistake when fighting someone my height—he aimed too high. I easily ducked under his swing, ignoring my pain, and slashed my dirk across his chest. My blade hit body armor and slid across, tearing his shirt.

Don't judge me. If I was fighting fabric, I'd be winning.

He saw his mistake and swung downward. I pivoted to one side and managed to cut his calf. It was a good shot and would slow him down, but he was far from out.

Using a classic fencing offense, he lunged his nightstick at my chest and I was helpless to do anything but take it. Pain reverberated through my body and I almost shut down. I would have, too, had it not been for Lizile's brew. Whatever it was, the stuff not only helped with the pain—it also blossomed new pain as well.

The Cherub had expected me to go down with his blow, like a real rookie, so he let his guard down. His arm was still extended—and unarmored—so I stabbed my dirk through his wrist.

He screamed like I'd ripped off his arm—pansy—and went down, cradling his wound. Not needing an invitation, I started to run.

Got pretty far, too, when I heard a *thud* and felt several ropes fly over my body and knock me down to the pavement. I tried to get up despite the pain, but something was weighing me down. That's when I realized I had been snared by a police net gun.

And just when I thought things were finally going my way.

↔

I tried to will myself unconscious as they dragged me over asphalt and gravel back to their truck. I almost *became* unconscious when they threw me in, my body literally bouncing as I hit the truck-bed floor. But I positively prayed to pass out when I saw my mother—also in a net—laying beside me with judgmental eyes that said:

You couldn't even get away, then?

Luckily, we were both too mad and in physical pain to talk.

Thank the GoneGods for small miracles.

Or don't. I don't care.

↔

They drove for three hours before finally pulling onto some dirt road and stopping, the truck sliding slightly on the gravel-covered earth. One of them got out and opened a squeaky gate. Then with the slamming of the truck door, he got back in and the truck moved on.

Because they'd covered us with a tarp, I had no idea where we were.

We could be anywhere, and when they finally stopped, pulling us out of the truck, I scanned our surroundings and noted a strange sight: several tree taps stuck in the bark of maple trees with blue hoses that ran from the taps into the warehouse. A maple syrup farm ... and given how rundown the taps were, I guessed we were on an old abandoned sugar farm.

My theory was confirmed when they dragged us into a large barn-like structure with a giant copper vat in the middle. Maple syrup—it was big business in the Laurentians, which meant that we were still in

Quebec. I filed that away in the "useful information should we not die" column.

The smallest of the three Cherubs bound us to a wooden beam in the center of the room with duct tape before sitting on a foldable chair nearby. The other two were going through our stuff and the largest of the three—Simione, from his accent—picked up my father's Cherub mask and brought it over to my mother.

"He loved you more than life itself." Then he pointed the mask at me. "You, too. 'Ma little angels,' he'd say. 'Ma reason for life itself.' Funny thing about that last statement—seems that your deaths were also his reason for life itself." Lifting his own mask enough to expose his mouth, he spat in my mother's face before going to the table with our stuff. "This, I also remember." Simione picked up my dirk. Stabbing the air in front of him, he said, "Your Eóghan stabbed many a monster with this."

"Simione," I said, "you don't have to do this. We're not the monsters we once were. Any of us."

"*IS THAT SO?!*" he shouted with such ferocity that both my mother and I flinched. " 'Not the monsters we once were.' *We*. WE?!" Then, taking a deep breath and unclenching his fists, he said, "We … once … were."

Um … clearly this guy had left his marbles at the bottom of the lake.

He walked right over to me so that his face was no more than a few inches away and pulled off his mask. "Tell me—when you look at me face, you don't think of monsters?"

I looked into crisp green eyes that were very human, as was the scar running above the left one … but that was the only part of him that was. The rest of his face was covered in crusty barnacles that created little craters a centimeter wide all across his face. The barnacle shells had imbedded themselves in his skin. In the few places beneath his chin where he had tried to remove them, I saw deep holes that could easily engulf my pinky finger. It must have hurt getting those out, and I guess after a few of them he stopped trying.

"They go all the way down, lassie," he said, removing his gloves and revealing hands that were more shell than skin. He gestured to his whole body, before stopping where his ... ah ... pride was. Then, thrusting his pelvis out, he said, "Either of you care for a ride on the barnacle express?"

At this the other two started laughing.

"Simione ..." I said, but my voice trailed off as words failed me.

He, on the other hand, had plenty of words left. "Do you know what your bitch of a mother did to me?"

I did, but the question seemed of the rhetorical variety, so I waited for him to give me a recap.

"She turned me into a vampire, locked me in a coffin—along with an arm and a leg and a few other scraps of what was left of my only friends in the world—and she threw us to the bottom of the Loch Ness. The last thing I heard besides the rushing water was, 'Say hi to Nessie for me.' If it hadn't been for the gods leaving and Nessie showing up in the loch with such a rush and force that it tore my coffin apart, I would have drowned."

GoneGodDamn, I thought. *My mother didn't just embrace evil. She* was *evil.* But then again, I couldn't help but think that in a way, I had done the same thing to my mother. I turned her and left her ... but I hadn't imprisoned her in a coffin and left her for the fishes—so, yay me?

Either way, I wasn't about to throw stones in glass houses. I was just going to stand in my glass house and hang my head in shame for all to see.

Still, looking at him, I couldn't blame the guy wanting revenge. Hell, I wanted to kill my mother for a lot less, and she never bound me and threw me in a lake.

My mother, sensing that there was nothing she could say to ease his anger, was uncharacteristically silent. I guess she didn't want to draw attention to herself. Smart move on her part, but it was quite a few decades too late.

Simione gave me a pursed, uneven smile, his barnacled lips together in such a way that it looked as though he had crooked teeth on the outside of his mouth. He waved the dirk in my face then walked over to the table and looked at the rest of our stuff.

157

It was mostly the contents of our combined purses. Lipsol, lipstick, lip gloss—a lot of lip stuff in general—and, of course, the amulet. "What's this?" he asked, picking it up to appraise it.

"Nothing," my mother said—a bit too eagerly.

"Nothing, huh?" He looked at it more closely before saying, "I tell you what—you give me the truth on this thing and I'll cut your suffering by, let's say, two hours. Sound fair?"

Neither of us spoke.

"*Don't* tell me and I'll increase your time on this Earth by three pain-fueled days." He lifted four fingers. Poor guy.

I considered my options. Tell him about an amulet that answers your biggest, most desired question—or don't. I figured that there was little harm in doing so—I doubted he cared where the gods went, anyway—and considered that if it distracted him from torturing us for a few minutes, well, that was a good thing, right?

"Ask it a question—"

"Darling. Shut up—"

"*YOU DON'T TALK, BITCH!*" he screamed. Then, looking at me and speaking in a voice that was calm and even: "Come again?"

"It will answer any question you ask it. So, ask away."

"Any question? Humph."

He turned the amulet over and over in his hand then turned to my mother. It was clear his voice was addressing the amulet.

"How should she die?"

Nothing happened. No noise, no change in the air, nothing. But something was happening for Simione—that much was obvious from the way his face turned from surprise to shock, and then to anger.

Whatever the answer was, it wasn't what he wanted to hear.

His rage manifested in him kicking the table over before slamming barnacle-covered hands against the wall in an all-out tantrum. The blow was severe enough to splinter the wood, and I could see from this vantage point that beneath his long-sleeved shirt were gears of some sort. So he *wasn't* super strong. He had one of those exoskeletons that augmented your strength. These exoskeletons were becoming increasingly standard issue for the military and police, which also explained the police-grade net gun from earlier. In a world filled with minotaurs, angels, draugars and hydras—all super strong—I guess you took any advantage you could get.

After several more punches, he stopped and, still breathing heavy, said, "Come with me. Now!"

The other two followed him outside, leaving my mother and I alone.

23

CONFESSIONS OF LOVE AND CONFESSIONS OF ... WELL, LET'S JUST SAY CONFESSIONS

hatever the amulet told Simione must have been bad—severe enough, at the very least, for him to leave my mother and me alone. Normally that would be a bad *James Bond* villain move, but I wasn't going to complain. We immediately tried to take full advantage by wiggling and worming, trying to get out of our damn bonds. But the duct tape held, and no amount of straining was going to free us. If we had a few hours, we might have been able to loosen the tape enough to free ourselves, but I could see the three of them just outside, discussing whatever evil plan they had in store for us. I knew it was futile.

Given how still my mother became, I guessed she came to the same conclusion. She confirmed it by saying, "It's no use."

So much for fighting to our last breath.

"Oh please, darling, that's the crap they try to sell us in movies. In the real world, most people realize when they're screwed and stop trying. You know that better than most."

I did—it always amazed me how many of my victims just stopped running. Granted, there was no hope. I was faster, immune to fatigue and relentless. But still, they'd just stop.

Stop ... and get to their knees.

Then they'd start to pray. To God or the gods. To angels and saints. Hell, a few of them prayed to their dearly departed mothers, asking them to come down from Heaven and save them.

And when their prayers were not answered (and I can tell you that in my three hundred years standing over countless victims, their prayers were never, ever answered—the gods may as well have never been here in the first place), they'd try another tact.

Begging.

When it became evident that begging was of no use, they'd go into terror mode—screaming and wailing—before (seconds before death, at this point) realizing that fear was useless. Everything was useless. They'd usually give into cursing, which always puzzled me—cursing their god or saint or dearly departed mother just moments after having prayed to the same. Then, once they got all that out of their system, they'd finally accept their fate with an often definite "Just do it" or "Get it over with."

And I would.

I call this the 7 Steps to Being Hunted and Caught:

1. Run
2. Stop
3. Pray
4. Beg
5. Terror
6. Cursing
7. Acceptance.

Damn. I should write a paper on that. Psych prof would love it.

The point is, none of them ever got away. Which isn't to say that some of them didn't survive my hunt. But it usually was the ones that kept their wits about them, thought their way through the problem and fought me off, or tricked me.

Those, and the truly lucky.

Everyone else was dinner.

I don't know where my mother and I were on the 7 Steps to Being

Hunted and Caught spectrum. I suppose our experience on the other side of the duct tape made us special cases—and we both just jumped straight to Acceptance.

What came after that, I wasn't sure.

But had I known, my underdeveloped sense of self-awareness would have done anything to *not* know.

↔

My mother let out a deep, mournful sigh and said, "I know what happened. To Simione."

"What?" I asked, wondering if we'd given up squirming too soon.

"He asked it the question—how I should die—and the amulet told him something else entirely. Probably unrelated to me. And from his reaction, something he didn't want to hear."

I tried to rotate my head enough to see my mother—not an easy feat, given that little Cherub duct taped my forehead to the beam. But with the little wiggle room I'd made for myself and using my periphery vision, I could see her out of the corner of my eye. "You asked it a question—didn't you?"

"I did," she said in a mournful voice.

"Did you ask it where the gods went?"

Silence.

"Mother ..."

More silence.

"We're going to die ... you might as well tell me. After all, what difference does it make?"

More silence. Just when I thought that she wasn't going to say anything, she whispered, "Because I don't want to die with you being angry at me."

I could see several tears escape her eye. So she really, truly didn't want me to know what she'd asked the amulet. And in our final moments on this Earth, I should have been understanding. Loving.

"It doesn't matter."

"Nae bother."

"I love you ..."

But curiosity, when it didn't kill the cat, did lead it down a dark and terrible path ... and I was *dying* to know. I wanted to know so badly that I might have died before Simione got a chance to kill me.

"Tell me," I said, and when my mother didn't answer, I tried a different tact. One that might have never occurred to me had I not met Mergen and seen the power of the Truth—capital T.

"Mother—of everything I have done in my life, I have three things that I would have changed had I not been so proud and ... well ... afraid."

I could almost *hear* my mother's curiosity. No dead cat this time. Not yet.

"The first one I won't tell you," I continued. "That is a story for another time. But number two of my oh-so-very-long list of regrets ... is turning you." I paused as I summoned the courage to say my third regret. "And number three is that once I turned you, I abandoned you. And for both those offences against you, I am truly and deeply sorry."

As soon as the words left my lips, I was struck by a very sudden and strong realization that I wasn't telling her this because I wanted to know her secret, but because I wanted her to know how sorry I was for what I had done to her.

I loved my mother as a human, hated her as a vampire ... and wasn't sure how I felt about her now that I was human again. All I did know was that I wanted to love her again. I wanted to be part of her life and have her be part of mine.

I also knew that I'd forgive her for whatever question she had asked the amulet. I didn't even have to hear it.

"Thank you, darling. Thank you for being so brave and so honest. I love you—"

"Whoa," I said. "Hey. I'm ready to forgive. And yeah ... to love. Not to talk about it. Gimme some space?"

My mother understood. Hell, she probably felt the same way—after all, the poisonous apple doesn't roll far from the cauldron.

There was a long silence between us, but unlike so much of the other kinds of silence that makes me uncomfortable, this one was pleasant. Daughter and mother, just enjoying a moment together … tied to a beam.

But blessed silence is only blessed for so long, and this moment we were having was broken by my mother's confession.

"You know," she started. "When the gods left, I actually went to church."

That was interesting. Vampires hated churches. We hated those places because, as strange as this sounds, light killed us. Sunlight burned us, but the light of spirituality and faith—that utterly devastated our beings.

"I gave confessional to a priest until …" She paused, searching for the right word. "Until I found my purpose in this GoneGod world."

"And what purpose is that?"

My mother ignored my question. "I found … no, we're being honest … I *find* being human so terribly hard. And not just me—I have met many ex-vampires and ex-weres that struggle. In many ways they have it harder than Others."

"I don't know about that—Others have it pretty hard."

"True," my mother said, "but everyone knows that an Other is an Other. They look at us and think we're a normal human just like them. They don't know what we were … and they don't understand what we gave up."

I silently agreed. Probably the hardest part of being human again was pretending that we were born—in my case—nineteen years ago and that we had a normal childhood and that we … well, we were like everyone else. The constant lying became tedious and tiresome, and atrophied our ability to move on with the rest of our lives.

But that wasn't what my mother was referring to. "What did we give up, Mother?"

I expected her to say the strength or speed or any number of other powers we had. What she said, though, truly shocked me.

"Faith," she sighed.

"Faith … as in, you know, faith in the guys who left us?"

"No, no, darling. Don't be daft. Faith in *myself*. Faith that no matter what happened, I was safe, that I was enough to deal with whatever life threw at me. Now I have a problem and I have no faith in myself to solve it. I just putter along, doing my best—"

"I think you're selling yourself a wee bit short. You were pretty spectacular at the diner and then at the Rust Yard. You're pretty badass, Mom."

"Humph—you called me Mom. You normally call me Mother—it's so formal. So impersonal."

I nodded (well, tried to). I let "Mom" slip every once in a while, but I usually defaulted to the formality. She was right. "You are pretty capable, Mom."

"Thank you, darling. Thank you … Kat," she said, and although I couldn't see her, I could sense her smile from her tone. "I guess that brings us to the point of this conversation … what question did I ask the amulet?"

"Mom—you don't have to—"

"No, you were right … let us clear the air before, well, you know."

And then she told me her question. And although I had promised myself I wouldn't get angry no matter what, my very being was consumed by a soul-fire of rage that the gods of peace from every religion the world ever knew could not temper.

24

SELFISH QUESTIONS, SELFISH BOYS

"*Y*ou asked it *WHAT?!*" I yelled.

"Darling, please, you'll draw those awful people back inside with your yelling."

"Mother, at this point I would welcome whatever horrible death they have in store for us than suffer another minute with *you*."

"Darling—you're being unreasonable."

"Am I?"

"Yes."

"How do you figure, Charlie?"

"Oh, please—you yourself admitted that being human was hard."

"I did—but as hard as it is, I'm not trying to find a way to become a vampire again!"

"Technically, darling, I'm trying to find the Soul Jar. There's a lot more I'll have to do to actually become a vampire. You have to figure out how to extract the soul from the body without killing it … then actually get the soul *into* the jar. And let's not forget that all of that doesn't guarantee our powers would come back just like that. We might just turn into these soulless husks with—"

"Shut up, shut up, shut up! I can't believe you actually want to become a vampire again. What about the rest of the shit you told me—all lies?"

"Like what?"

"The organization you work for."

"Mmm, more like a support group for ex-vampires. We're quite large. National, actually."

"And who did I speak to? It wasn't the President."

"Ah, that … yes, you were the victim of our little play, I'm afraid. You *did* speak to the president, technically."

"Of the United States?"

"Of our organization. Interesting fellow. Raspy voice, though. Did you know he was one of the first Grand Inquisitors—"

"And the whole 'keep the amulet out of people's hands to protect the secret of where the gods went'?"

"That was true! We really are concerned about it falling into the wrong hands and causing an ideological problem for the world."

"*You* are the wrong hands!"

"Oh, pish posh," she said in her usual derivative tone. But just when I thought she'd go into some tirade or other, her voice became very somber, and I sensed true remorse in her voice. "Besides," she said in barely a whisper, "it didn't work."

"What didn't?"

Now my mother started crying. And I don't mean a couple conservative tears, I mean proper tears. Twice in one day. I was speechless.

"My question," she said between sniffs. "I asked the damn thing where the Soul Jar is, and I had another question answered altogether. Do you want to know what question it answered?"

I took several deep breaths as I tried to come to grips with the fact that my mother was part of some scheme to *restore* humans back to their former vampiric selves. She wanted to bring back the blood sucking and hunting, the torturing and hurting, the power and … what was the word she used … *faith in herself.*

That last thought tempered my rage just enough for me to realize that maybe my mother hadn't considered all the consequences of finding a way back to vampirehood. She didn't think about all the new innocent victims that would suffer in the GoneGod world.

She was just thinking about herself.

I took several deep breaths and considered my next words when, finally calm enough, I heard what my mother was muttering over and over again in between sobs and tears.

"Do you want to know what question it answered?

"Do you want to know what question it answered?

"Do you want to know what question it answered?"

I couldn't take it anymore and with a resigned huff, I said, "Yes. *Please* tell me—what question did it answer?"

My mother took a deep breath, evidently trying to get her tears under control. "What I want most in this new GoneGod world. Do you want to know what that is?"

"Yes, Charlie," I said, hoping she'd hear me rolling my eyes.

"It was—"

"Oye ... what you two blabbering on about?" yelled one of the Cherubs.

I guess I wasn't going to find out what my mother desired more than anything. Given that it was probably a castle or unlimited wealth or a harem of Chippendale dancers, I wasn't too concerned. I was ready for my death to end this.

↔

Two of them came back without Simione and took off their masks. I could see why they joined the Divine Cherub club—they were both hideous. The smaller one looked like a battered version of Ringo Starr (it was uncanny—let the conspiracy theories abound) and the larger of the two had a George Harrison vibe going for him. But not the cute, early-days George. He was the skinny, mustache-wearing, bad-haircut George of the 1970s. (Believe me, I know

George—he was my favorite Beatle, pre- *and* post-Yoko. I like the quiet types.)

George walked up to me and did probably the creepiest thing a guy can do to a tied-up girl—he sniffed me. Yuck.

"George—what are you doing?" Evidently, he didn't just *look* like George—he was *named* George. And who said the gods didn't have a sense of humor (when they were around, that is)?

"Just taking a whiff."

"Simione said not to touch them."

"I know," George said, clearly irritated. "But Simione isn't here, is he?"

"Where is he?" I asked, figuring I had nothing to lose by asking.

"Oh, oh, oh, he's gone to get something very special for you two," George chuckled. "Very, very special."

"Like what?" I asked.

"And ruin the surprise?" he said.

"Good point," I said. "We like surprises, don't we, Mother?"

"I don't think we'll like this one, darling." Evidently, she wasn't in a mood for playing around.

George took another sniff and ran the back of his hand along my cheek. It took all my strength not to shudder. "Probably not. But then again, who knows what kind of kinky stuff you sluts are into?"

Seriously—is this guy really trying to chat me up here and now? And with a word like "slut" to boot. Who is this guy? Magna cum laude from porn school?

They both chuckled at this.

Speaking rather than just thinking out loud, I said, "So when will he be back?"

Remember what I said about the 7 Steps of Being Hunted and Caught? Those guys never survived. It was the ones who maintained their calm—who could form a plan. And I was beginning to form a plan of my own.

"A couple hours," George said.

"And then what? Curtains for us? If so, maybe you'd honor me by making my last few hours a little bit more comfortable. I'd be ever so grateful." I turned on my sultry, bring-it-on voice ... the one I reserved for nights when I was feeling particularly adventurous.

" *'Curtains for us'?* Who talks like that? Oh yeah, vampire bitches who think everyone is stupid but them." He punched me in the gut, which hurt way more than it should have given my whole ribs situation.

"Too far?" I asked, my voice just a groan.

"Too much like a porn," he said. "Remember, I'm one of their best students."

So not as stupid as I hoped. GoneGodDammit!

Out of plans—and apparently not as seductive as I thought I was— I had no clue what to do next, so I fell into silence and did what I always did when I was trapped: I started to play a movie in my head. It was a technique I learned to do from a yogi in one of the most sacred of places—SoHo. If you've never been, go. The experience will positively enlighten you.

I was running through my playlist when my mother decided to ruin my last hours of life. "You know, George, you weren't far off by calling my daughter a slut. In fact, this whole predicament we find ourselves in is because she couldn't keep her hormones in check. Isn't that true, darling?"

This was a surprise. And insulting. "What are you getting at, Mother?"

"Gareth? The cèilidh? Fornicating on the bluff near the loch in the middle of night? Remember that?"

"I do, Mother, but I was a victim."

"Were you? Or were you inviting this curse on yourself because you were a selfish little girl? Are *still* a selfish little girl?"

"Mother—this is hardly the time for—"

"And once you were turned, you couldn't just leave us alone. You killed me, and don't think for one second, missy, that I don't know what you did to your father."

I stopped, my eyes widening. Did she know? I hadn't told her what happened, I haven't told anyone ... I couldn't possibly see how she would know.

Whether I said that out loud or not, my mother went on. "You killed him. By fang or because you set him on his impossible mission to save the world from monsters like you, you killed him."

So, she didn't know. I breathed a sigh of relief. Ouch—my ribs.

"And that's not all, darling … you did so without a care in the world."

This last comment pissed me off. I cared. In fact, it was *because* I cared that he died. I was trying to rebuild our family. I was trying to make us whole. That's why I turned him. How was I to know that he'd choose watching the sun rise one final time over living forever? With me. With us. I watched him turn to dust and there wasn't a damn thing I could do about it. That was my biggest regret, the one I couldn't tell Mother … and her cruel words were forcing me to relive the most painful moment of my life.

"You selfish little brat," she said. "You—"

It was all too much and I started to wiggle and writhe. I couldn't hear another word. Not one more word. My arms and legs were still caught against the duct tape, but unlike the first time I tried to pry myself free, this time … the tape broke.

↔

I managed to rip myself off of the beam in one fluid motion, and as I tore free, I saw my mother do the same. I looked over to see her fingers bleeding and a piece of splintered wood clutched in them. She had used her time, not only chatting with me, but whittling us free from the tape.

Not wanting to waste what my mother had done, I immediately tackled George. I had expected to meet resistance, but he wasn't ready for me to charge and had toppled over.

And now that I knew the source of his strength, I didn't waste time trying to match his, but rather ran my hands on the elbow joints of his armor and pulled.

It took everything I had, but I managed to bend the joint just enough to render his arm useless—and in a lot of pain.

I saw my mother do the same to the other Cherub.

Leaping forward, I grabbed my father's mask and dirk and tossed my mother one of their telescopic nightsticks.

We headed for the door.

My mother leapt through the window.

Running up the hill and away from the sugar farm, I expected my mother to do the same thing. What I didn't expect was for her to run around the front—probably to find me—only to be hit by a truck that had been coasting down the hill with its lights off.

I guess our two hours were up.

25

THE LESSER OF TWO RIGHTS

I watched with horror from the top of the hill as Simione
and the other two bound my mother—this time in chains—
and took her and the truck near the dock, where a hand-powered
crane used for lowering things into the lake stood. His minions
started to unload the truck. Evidently, if Simione was going to come
after me, it wasn't going to be now. I guessed he figured he had a life-
time to hunt me down.

Instead, he pulled out several clear, plexiglass sheets, metal fasten-
ings and a bunch of tools. It didn't take long for me to realize that he
was building a glass box large enough for two humans to stand
comfortably inside. As I watched him unload an old diver's mask—the
kind you found in the 1950s, complete with an apparatus used for
pumping air down to the mask—I understood his plan.

Drop my mother down in the lake.

And supply her with just enough air that she wouldn't drown.

And when I saw the diving suit and fins, I realized that he meant to
visit her from time to time to ... what? ... feed her? Take care of her?
Keep her alive? Regardless of all this effort, she wouldn't survive long
down there. Still, he was doing enough that her death would be slow
and painful. And awful.

I considered my next move. I could run up the main road, find my way back to the nearest town and call for help. Of course, help would come in the form of an ex-were and changeling. Possibly an avatar, too.

But by the time they showed up, my mother would have been down there for hours, if not a full day.

Then I had one of the most horrible thoughts of my life … and I've thought of some truly evil shit.

Leave my mother.

Let her die.

If anyone deserved it, she did. Simione alone was proof of that. Vampire or not … what she did to him was beyond our vampiric nature. It was downright evil.

I could just walk away and prepare for Simione's inevitable attack. Ready for him—and with the help of my friends, he didn't stand a chance.

As they wrapped chains around her and prepared the glass coffin, I thought, *I could wash my hands of my mother once and for all.*

↔

But I couldn't do that. Despite whatever evil she did before, she deserved a second chance to be human. As misguided a human as she may be, and even if she didn't *want* to be human … she still deserved a chance.

Besides, her question hadn't been answered, which meant that her greatest desire *wasn't* to become a vampire again. It was something else. Something very selfish, I was sure, but at least she didn't truly want to go back to the killing and blood sucking and all that terrible stuff.

So how would I save my mother against three wannabe Divine

Cherubs? Two were hurt, their strength armor incapacitated, but there was still three against one. I needed a plan. I needed a—

I needed some sugar.

↔

OK—I didn't really need sugar. I was more after the equipment used to make maple syrup.

You see, when I was a young vampire, about forty years undead, I traveled to the far east to study under a master. And by "master," I don't mean vampire—generally, vampires weren't the supportive bunch.

I mean Grand Master of the Martial Arts.

What kind? I don't know its name, and I ate the Grand Master before he could expand his dojo and teach other humans (another regret on that long list I was talking about). He taught me many things, but the one lesson that has always been truly effective was how to use the terrain against your enemy.

And that was exactly what I was going to do now.

Sneaking down to the warehouse, I quietly turned on every maple sap tap on all the maple trees in the area. There were a lot of them, but because I couldn't turn on the pumps, the maple wouldn't flow very fast (and maple sap is more water than sugar, so it's not very sweet or sticky). But those taps had been closed for a while now, which meant there was some sap ready to get out; given how many taps there were, the vats within the refinery would fill up pretty quickly as well.

Then I waited. Anything I was going to do would be done at dawn … the worst time for a vampire to fight, but also the time that Simione and his motley band of morons would least expect an attack from me. They'd figure my vampiric nature would dictate an attack at night or no attack at all. Their guard would be down and they'd be exhausted.

Well, the other two would be exhausted—Simione seemed to be reenergized by preparing my mother's watery coffin. From my vantage point I could see the care that he was taking in making sure the sealing was right, the pumps would work and that everything would go according to plan.

This did strike me as odd, because he wanted to *kill* my mother. If things didn't go as planned, she'd drown and ... well ... mission accomplished. But from the way he checked the equipment again and again, I realized that he wanted to torture my mother more than he wanted to kill her. In a strange way, I think he'd be more upset if she died quickly than if she got away. At least escape meant that he'd have a chance to hunt her down and start all over. Besides, being hunted is a type of torture. He'd relish in the knowledge that she was constantly looking over her shoulder for him.

The other thing that struck me as odd was that in all his preparation, he never actually touched her. Never raised a hand. Hell, he never even raised his voice—a true sign of restraint for him. From where I was watching, I knew he was talking to her, but for the life of me, I couldn't hear a word.

Whatever he was saying, my mother was crying. As much as she deserved this, Simione was going to pay extra for making her cry a *third* time.

↔

As the first sunlight began to peek out, I got into position. There were a couple of things I needed to do before I could announce my presence, and with the cover of morning birds chirping, I made my moves.

The first thing I did was collect a bucketful of sap from one of the shut-off vats. They hadn't filled as much as I'd hoped, but there was enough sap in the massive copper pots to drown a person—if he laid perfectly still, face down.

The next part would be the hard part. Uncapping the truck's fuel lid, I poured in half the bucket. I got inside, popped the truck's parking brake and put the damn anti-environment truck-a-saurus into Neutral and let it coast down the hill with me inside.

So it begins.

It rolled down and toward the warehouse. I heard a gratifying "What the fuck?" followed by a "Go get my truck!" in a very distinct Inverness-circa-1730s accent. Then one of the idiots came running after it.

At the speed the truck was going, the crunch I heard meant that the truck crashed into one of the copper vats at such a low velocity it didn't even crack the thing open.

Perfect.

Next, the running idiot jumped into the driver's seat.

The other thing my Master told me was to use the hierarchy against them. A general would always send a grunt to do grunt work and, as expected, the Ringo-looking Cherub was sent to retrieve the truck. He'd be the most inexperienced and, therefore, the least likely to actually check the truck's backseat.

As soon as he tried the engine—which churned and groaned as the sugar made its way into the engine block—I wrapped one of those blue hoses used to bring in the sap to tie back his arm and wrapped a second one around his neck.

It was tricky getting the two hoses over him at once, but I'd done this particular move many times before and it amazed me how muscle memory kicked in all these years later. It was like riding a bike—a murderous, psychotic bike.

He gagged as he tried to struggle free, and from the rearview mirror I could see the terror in his eyes as his life left him. He was terrified of dying. Aren't we all? But if he had a bit more experience, he would have realized he wasn't dying at all. If you're going to choke someone to death, you want something thin that will cut into the skin. But that's only if you wanted to kill them. I didn't. I just wanted to knock him out.

If I could avoid it, I would never kill again. The operative words in that statement being *If I could avoid it*. I'd never taken an oath, made a solemn swear and pledged to lead a kill-free life. I had spent too long as a vampire to see the role that death plays in life to make such a bold claim. I believe my Psychology Prof would say I was "exhibiting good self-awareness." I would, however, try my best. By using a flat, plastic hose, I would cut off the airway enough that eventually he'd pass out.

It took a minute, but eventually he was out. Tying the rope tightly against the seat, I honked the horn, rolled out of the truck, shimmied up to a new hiding spot ... and waited.

If hierarchal protocol dictated anything, George would be the next to come through ... and I had a plan for him, too.

But protocol wasn't adhered to, because both of them came running inside.

Perfect. Just as I had expected.

↔

Simione was no idiot, and I knew he was no idiot. He didn't send in Ringo to get the truck because he was the bottom of the ladder; he sent him ahead because he was the first in the cannon-fodder line. In other words, Simione sent him in to spring whatever trap I had set. If the truck had rolled down by accident, then no harm. But if it was a trap, then best have the smallest and most insignificant of the crew spring that trap. And once the trap was sprung, they'd come in with force and deal with the problem once and for all.

It's what I'd do.

Simione and George ran in just as I had expected. What I hadn't expected was that as he ran in, he cried out, "Katrina, my lass, please do not waste my time. Your mother—she is about to take the ... uh ... *plunge* and I desperately do not want to miss it."

Shit. I had expected his desire to watch her go under to stop him from doing anything until he was in the clear to savor the moment.

But he had used the hand crane to put her in the water while I was dealing with Ringo.

Taking a second, I looked out the window. Not only did I see my mother bobbing in the glass coffin like an ice cube, but she didn't have any head gear on.

The bastard was going to let her drown.

Simione had just raised the stakes: either I had to make my move and quickly to save my mother, or she'd drown. He was forcing my hand.

Shit! Shit-shit-shit, GoneGodDammit!

But he'd also raised the stakes on himself, too. All that effort to torture her, lost. All that pent-up desire to watch her die slowly, gone. All I had to do to ruin his plans was take my time.

That's exactly what I did.

I waited.

"Come out, Kat, lest your mother drowns."

I didn't do anything.

"Come on, dearie," he said. I could sense the urgency begin to rise in his voice.

I still didn't move. I had expected that I, too, would be anxious, wanting to get to my mother and save her ... but if I'm being honest (and Mergen would appreciate that), doing nothing was easier than I thought.

"Katrina! She'll die and—damn it all to hell! Go, go!"

I heard George run outside, then an exasperated sigh from Simione.

"OK, you got me, you clever, cheeky little girl. I would never kill your mother. Well, I'd never kill her *quickly*. I should have known you'd understand that. We are, after all, cut from the same cloth, are we not?"

I don't know what cloth he's talking about, but mine is decidedly barnacle free, I thought—making sure that one was in my head.

"We're both *more than* killers, because we both like to play with our prey—rhyme intended." As he spoke, I could hear him walking around the warehouse looking for me.

I had picked my hiding place well; I wouldn't be easy to find. And given how sparse this place was, I suspected that he might think I wasn't in the warehouse at all. One could hope.

From the sound of his footsteps, I could tell that he was walking close to the large vat in the center. Once he got within a couple feet of the thing, I could see him in all his barnacled glory.

Perfect ... just a little bit closer ...

He leaned over—and that's when I pounced.

↔

I knew I couldn't beat him with sheer force. He was too strong. But his strength came from the armor he wore, not from natural abilities or from magic. Which meant there were chinks in his armor that couldn't be filled.

I'd read up a bit about these exoskeletons in the news. The biggest complaint about the armor was the spine, because as much as you could enhance someone's arms and legs, and even grip, you couldn't make their lower back stronger. Reinforced—yes. But physically stronger—no.

Which meant that to win, I'd have to hurt his back. So, when he leaned over to investigate the light noises that the dripping of the maple sap made, I had my chance.

I'd been hiding in the rafters just above the vat. Now, leaping down feet first, I forced his upper torso into the vat, flipping him over so that his lower half stayed outside. I also made sure that my left foot fell onto his lower back—and secretly hoped it left a boot print, just like his had on my blouse.

I had worried about the vat holding, but hoped it would—after all, it was meant to hold in a couple thousand gallons of maple syrup.

I heard the snap, followed by a scream, and I knew I had won.

Against *him*, at least.

There was still George and my mother to worry about.

↔

I left Simione draped over the copper vat's wall and ran outside to help my mother. George was reeling her back in using the hand crank. As soon as he saw me standing there, he probably thought that Simione was dead and Ringo was going to eventually get out of his bonds to help.

He released the hand crank and my mother's casket plopped back into the water, bobbing up and down much faster than she had when I was in the warehouse. I guess the glass cage had taken on a lot of water already. She would go down quickly.

My momentary distraction on my mother was enough time for George to do what any good foot soldier does when his general is downed—run.

He ran up the hill and away. The huntress in me wanted to chase after him and stake him to a maple tree so that sap would drizzle out of his nose. But the more-evolved me ran to the water's edge to save my mother.

My Psychology prof would say that I was exhibiting signs of *improvement*.

I need to get this woman's voice out of my head, I thought in my head.

By the time I got to shore, the cage was already submerged. I needed another tactic if I was going to save dear ol' Mama. I bee-lined to the dock and grabbed Simione's air tank, weight belt and regulator.

Using the belt to force the air tank to submerge, I swam down to my mother. The side of the case had a little latch and door just big enough for a Simione-sized human to swim through. That's exactly what I did. Then, placing the regulator in my mother's mouth, I waited until she sucked in a couple deep breaths before taking it back. While she breathed, I worked on loosening her facets.

181

After about thirty rounds of back-and-forth breathing, I freed her.

We swam up to shore, dragging our sorry, tired butts out of the water. We were still hugging each other, and once we were on shore, neither of us let go. Lying on the lake's poor excuse for a beach, we soaked in the air, the sun and the simple, pleasant fact that we were alive.

Not dead, not *undead ... alive.*

Neither of us spoke, enjoying being in each other's arms for the first time in a very long time indeed.

↔

But alas, all good things must end to make room for other things—not always pleasant. Or good. Or even understandable.

Wet, cold and tired, my chest still burning in pain, we made our way back to the warehouse. Ringo was awake now but hadn't managed to break free. I got into the back of the truck and made sure that he'd never get loose. Not without help. Or suddenly developing super powers.

My mother was by Simione's side, but neither of them were speaking. I had expected my mother to gloat. That was her style. But she didn't say anything, just stared down at the hunched man, shaking her head.

I joined her and once we closed the vat, I saw that Simione wasn't speaking because Simione was dead. Drowned in about three inches of sap. The man must have realized that he'd lost ... that he'd probably never walk again, too, considering what I'd done with his exoskeleton ... and that he'd never get his revenge. He chose death over suffering.

Staring down at him, I found a strange admiration for the crazed man. The willpower alone to force himself to stay underwater. The sheer determination.

I didn't know if I could ever do that—I still don't know—no matter how bad it got.

Bending over, I closed his lifeless eyes. *This was a good way to go*, I thought, *for after a few hundred years of not drowning, I guess going that way was poetic in its own, twisted way.*

"I don't know, darling," my mother said. "I don't think any way is a good way to go."

2 6

ONE LAST CONFESSION

*M*y mother didn't want to call the police, preferring to hide the bodies in the forest. I pointed out that Ringo was still alive and she gave me a *So what?* shrug.

I believe my Psychology prof would say she was *regressing*.

Good thing, though—I wasn't. I calmly explained that we would use one of the Cherubs' cell phones to get the cops here and then leave —but only after we cleaned up the crime scene of any evidence we were ever here.

I also explained to Ringo that mentioning either of our names to the cops would result in him being hunted down and ... well, he could use his imagination; sometimes the best threats are the ones the threatenee comes up with in their own head.

His emphatic nodding showed that he understood perfectly. And that he had a vivid imagination.

Then, grabbing one of their backpacks, I filled it with the four Cherub masks and dirk. I also made sure to put the amulet in my pocket. My mother saw me do it and said nothing.

I had considered taking one of the strength-enhancing exoskeletons for myself, but that meant disrobing either Ringo or Simione. I wouldn't touch Simione, for obvious reasons ... and Ringo was already bound. Besides, the fact that they were both in body armor would help add to the confusion of the crime scene—and right now that was the best thing we had going for us. Hell, I doubted they acquired the tech legally from the government. Cops tended to close cases after making arrests.

We called the cops and trekked up the hill toward the closest town, which was only the GoneGods knew how far.

↔

The closest town, it turned out, was only a three-hour hike, but by the time we got there we were beat and near collapsing. We found a diner where I used the payphone—thank the GoneGods they still had one— to call Egya, who dutifully borrowed Justin's car to come get us. It would take him two hours to get to us—I guess we didn't get very far after all.

My mother and I tried to talk while we waited. Mostly she complained that we should have used the Cherub's cell phone, and I pointed out that we hadn't known where we were, and leaving my friend's phone number on a phone belonging to the bad guys who would probably be under investigation was a terrible idea with far-reaching consequences. She gave me a weak "pish posh" before falling into silence and, upright in her chair, sleep.

Later I'd learn that George was less of a coward than I thought. He had circled back to free Ringo, and when the police eventually showed up, all they found was an abandoned truck.

I guess the two good foot soldiers buried their general. I hoped, at least.

If they were to come after my mother and I? We'd deal with them then.

But I didn't know any of that while sitting in the diner that day. All

I did know was my mother was asleep and I was drowning in coffee, waiting for Egya to show up and rescue me.

↔

Almost exactly two hours later, Egya showed up in my boyfriend's Mustang, his smile wider than ever. We got in and he drove us to the gas station to find my mother's smashed-up, rented Prius.

"Leave me here, darling," my mother said. "I'll call AAA or something. Thank the GoneGods I got the extra insurance."

And without another word, she got out of the car.

She got out of the car.

Out of the car—without saying another word.

Oh, hell no!

I got out and, exhausted or not, stomped up to my mother. "We nearly died, your quest was foiled and all you can say is 'Thank the GoneGods I got the extra insurance'?"

"What else did you want me to say, darling?" she asked, lifting a curious eyebrow.

"I don't know—thank you, or goodbye, or ... I don't know!"

I believe my Psychology prof would say I was looking for closure.

Maybe I was starting to get the hang of this "human" thing. And maybe, just maybe, it was enough to pass that damn class.

Standing there, I waited patiently for my mother to say the wrong thing and for me to rush off in a huff back into the car with a dramatic "Drive, Egya. Just drive."

But my mother didn't say the wrong thing. She actually said the right thing—for once.

Taking my hand in hers, she kissed my cheeks before giving me a hearty hug. "Do you know what Simione was saying to me as he built that glass coffin? Just four words, over and over again. 'She's not coming back.' That was it. I guess he knew exactly what to say to hurt me the most. 'She's not coming back.' But you did, darling. You did. Thank you."

"Well, someone had to save you," I said, hugging her back.

She pulled away and shook her head. "Oh no, darling. That's not why I'm thanking you."

"Then what for?"

She kissed my cheeks again and stared at me for a long moment as she contemplated saying something. I could see the debate in her eyes before she finally shook her head. "I never told you what the amulet spoke. I asked it where the Soul Jar was ... and it told me that my heart desired the answer to a very different question. Do you want to know?"

"Mother ... Mom ... do we have to? I'm too tired to get into a fight with you."

"I am, too. But I don't think the question my heart asked will anger you. It might *upset* you, but anger is not the reaction I suspect you'll have."

"OK—what did your heart ask?"

"Let us just say that whatever the question was, the amulet's words came true. Well ... have *started* to come true." She pulled me in for another hug.

With that done, she guided me to the mustang and opened the door. "Take care of my little girl," she said to Egya with a wink.

The Ghanaian didn't say anything, just giving her a solemn nod before placing his right fist over his heart—a gesture common for his tribe that meant he would do all he could.

"Good," she said as she squeezed my hand. "Katrina. I never told you what I am thankful to you for."

"Mom ... I don't know if I have it in me for any more emotions. I'm kind of tapped out—"

"Pish posh, darling. You will indulge your mother one last word."

She stood up, adjusted her now dry, but very wrinkled outfit before nodding to herself and looking at me.

"I am thankful to you because you have given me hope, Katrina.

And not only hope ... for the first time in a long time, I'm not so afraid."

↔

With that, we drove off, back to university and all the problems being human entailed. And, of course, chief amongst them was Justin. With a heavy sigh, I walked to his dorm room like one might walk to the gallows.

The conversation between us was horrible. I cried. He cried. I wanted to run away and from the number of times he got up and walked to the door, so did he. But he always stopped himself, turning around and asking that next question. And the next.

I answered them all as truthfully as I could. No more lies. No more secrets.

And when it was over, we were both exhausted.

We slept together that night. No sex (not that that had happened yet), no kissing. We didn't even cuddle. We just slept next to each other and when the morning light woke us up, I turned to the boy who (*whom,* my mother would say) I cared for deeply—the boy I might love—with expecting eyes.

Eyes that turned away from me.

"I'm sorry, Kat," he said. "I just don't know."

"About what?" I asked.

Stupid question, but if it was over, I had to hear him say it.

"I just don't know if I ... if we can work. You are so ..." His voice trailed off.

No amount of willpower or control stopped my emotions from showing themselves. As my tears betrayed me, I reached out my hand for his.

He did not reach back.

I nodded. I stood up and headed for the door. It was time for me to go. I had told him everything. I had spoken the Truth, my Truth, knowing full well what the consequences might be. He had heard me and chosen not to be with me.

So be it.

"Experienced," he said.

I had expected the words *evil, wrong, tainted* ... but *experienced*?

I turned around. "Excuse me?"

His gaze was far away, like he was struggling with something. I waited, patiently willing him to speak again.

When he did, he said, "You are older than my great, great, great, great grandmother. And you have done so much. I just don't know how to be with someone like you."

"And the vampire stuff. You know—blood sucking and all?"

"That, too. I don't know how I feel about that. It's all so confusing." He stood up and took my hand in his. "What I do know is I like you for who you are ... not who you *were*. And you aren't that person anymore. Are you?"

I shook my head. I wasn't. I really wasn't.

"But ..." He pulled his hand away. "I just don't know."

"So, what now?"

"I ..." He paused, looking down into my eyes. "I think we go back to what you told me that night we first kissed."

"How I've never been so close to a boy before and *not* wanted to rip out his throat?"

Justin didn't laugh.

"Too soon?"

"Yes," he confirmed, then shook his head. "That other thing you said. About taking it slow. Dating. Being an *item*."

"Oh, yeah—that. OK. I can do that. Let's start over." I stuck out my hand. "Hi. I'm Katrina Darling. Ex-vampire, freshman and totally confused."

He took my hand. "Hi. I'm Justin Truly. Always-human, junior and totally confused as well."

And right there lay our common thread.

We were both struggling to be human.

. . .

↔

Over the next couple of days, things returned to normal. I took my Psychology test and by some miracle that was Egya's incredible notes, I passed. Barely.

Still, I guess I'm not as bad at being human as I thought.

Deirdre and I went to the Rust Yard to visit the mutated pups. They were just fine, running around the lot happy as mutated rats could be.

And as for my mothe—mom. She figured out Skype and regularly Skype sniped me ... So I heard from her a lot. And I didn't mind. Much.

As the weekdays turned to weekend, we all decided to have dinner at Mama's. We heard the glass window had been repaired and we felt we owed her our patronage, given the kind of riff-raff we attracted. We met outside, Justin opting to walk instead of drive this time, and stood awkwardly out front. This was the first time the three of us had been together since the kidnapping.

"Let's dine," Egya said with his usual uncompromising smile.

"You guys go ahead," I said, scanning the street. "I need a minute."

They went inside, Justin pausing to ask if everything was OK.

"I just need a minute to soak it all in. It's been a hell of a week."

He nodded as if understanding and walked in.

Alone, I scanned the street. In the last week, I'd unburdened myself of a lot of ... what was the clinical term? ... baggage. I told Justin, crafted an uneasy peace with my mother and passed my test. Things were looking up.

Trouble with me and being optimistic ... I always waited for the other shoe to drop (whatever that means). In other words, I was always looking for a reason to be miserable, no matter how happy I was.

Well, that will have to change, I thought in a glass-half-full sort of way. *People change. I can change. I can be happy without worrying what tomorrow will be.*

And with that I turned on my heel, put on the biggest smile I could muster and walked inside.

I was happy.

Still ... I couldn't shake the feeling that I was being watched.

Probably just the empty half of the glass protesting.

Probably.

27
THE RASP

ATE EVENING—

It has been so long since he's hunted. So long since he's stalked his prey. And now that he has her in his sights, he wonders if she is the right target to begin with. After all, there are so many others who would be easier marks to take down.

So many to hunt.

He shakes this thought out of his head. *Best to take down difficult prey first*, he thinks. *She is the most dangerous—and beyond that, I am a hunter whose skills are rotting. To test myself against simple, easy prey is to be defeated before I even begin. No, I must regain my instincts, refine my skills.*

I must become the hunter I once was.

Assured that she—Katrina Darling—is, indeed, the right prey, he stands on top of this old, abandoned cinema, watching as she and her friends enter the diner across the street. They are laughing, preparing to enjoy a carefree meal … and completely unaware that they are being stalked.

As Katrina follows her friends inside, the hunter remarks to himself how young she is.

He quickly dismisses the thought. He's a fool to entertain such sentiments. Miss Darling is not young. She is a three-hundred-year-old vampire, made human again. And not because she sought to regain her humanity or expelled the vampire virus through some kind of ritual or magic. No, she was made human again against her will.

She was made human when the gods left, taking their magic with them. She is human again—completely against her will.

Human or not, he reminds himself, *she is still dangerous*. She has years of experience as a huntress. Years of knowledge on how to kill. Decades of practice using both supernatural and natural skills alike to take down her prey.

She is dangerous. Very dangerous, he remarks to himself with a smile.

"Good," he said in a raspy, unsettling voice. "So am I."

ALSO BY RAMY VANCE

Mortality Bites Series

Mortality Bites

Family Matters

Superhero Me!

Orphaned Follies

Dawn of a Thousand Sunsets

Three Dead Gods

Run, Kat, Run

Encantado Dreams

The Heaviest of Burdens

Looking for a great deal? Grab these book bundles...

Setting Fires with Dragons - complete series

Mortality Bound - complete series

GoneGod World - Complete series

Series Starter - Bundle

ALSO BY RAMY VANCE

Mortality Bites Series

Mortality Bites

Family Matters

Superhero Me!

Orphaned Follies

Dawn of a Thousand Sunsets

Three Dead Gods

Run, Kat, Run

Encantado Dreams

The Heaviest of Burdens

Looking for a great deal? Grab these book bundles...

Setting Fires with Dragons - complete series

Mortality Bound - complete series

GoneGod World - Complete series

Series Starter - Bundle